CW01511783

A FAMILY FOR CHRISTMAS: A REGENCY ROMANCE

ROSE PEARSON

A FAMILY FOR CHRISTMAS:
A REGENCY ROMANCE

CHAPTER ONE

I t seemed strange, on such a somber occasion as a funeral, that there were boughs of holly, hundreds of candles and garlands of evergreens decorating the church ready for the service to commemorate the beginning of Advent that was due to take place the next day. Anna Campbell looked at the coffin set upon trestles at the altar. It contained the mortal remains of her father, Colin Campbell. The casket was the best she could afford—and had been the cheapest the carpenter could offer. Anna ran a hand over the rough, unvarnished wood and wondered if she would miss him at all.

The vicar's words echoed around the empty church as he performed the final blessing and said a solemn prayer commending Pa to God's mercy. He gave Anna a rueful smile, then nodded to the men hovering at the very back of the church to come and fetch the coffin to take it to the gravesite. They were clad in dark clothes, their boots and breeches covered with mud. They had swarthy complexions from working outside in all weathers. Their expressions were solemn and inscrutable. She could only assume that they were the gravediggers and that the vicar had paid them a few coppers more to come and carry Pa to the gravesite as she had nobody who might do it for her. She nodded to them politely, and they gave her a respectful half-bow, then another to the casket, before they picked it up and began to walk steadily down the aisle.

Anna followed them, the vicar walking just ahead of them all as they carried her father's body towards the doors of the church. The pews were all empty. There was not a soul present to witness Pa's passing or to offer Anna their love and support. It did not surprise Anna that not even one of the more dedicated members of the congregation had come, as they often would for even a stranger that was to be buried. Pa had made too many enemies in his life for anyone to mourn him, much less offer him respect, and she hadn't known if there was anyone she should have told that he had finally succumbed to the evils his whoring, drinking, and gambling had put upon his body. She doubted that even she would miss him.

There was an aunt somewhere. Anna's mother's sister. There had been no contact between them since long before Anna had been born, so she doubted that even they, her only family now, would have wanted to come and pay their respects. Pa had always grumbled that Mama's high-and-mighty sister had never thought Pa good enough—it had always been clear that there was little love lost between them. All Anna knew of Aunt Hannah was her mother's stories of their childhood and the moments when it was clear just how much she missed her sister after Hannah had upped and left home to marry a man who lived in some grand city somewhere. It might have been London, or Liverpool, York, or even Edinburgh. It had never been spoken of, and Anna had been too young to remember the details—Ma had died when Anna was barely five years old, and all she had been left with was an idea that someday she might seek out her aunt so that she could get away from her miserable life with Pa.

The silent quartet made their way out of the church. The weather was mild but damp, making everything smell just a little earthy. The churchyard was sheltered by trees and filled with extravagant monuments to the much-beloved dead. Anna admired the beauty of some of the carvings and sculptures that adorned the graves of the wealthy, buried as close to the church as they could be. She noted the way the extravagance of the closest graves gave way to simple headstones and unadorned crosses as they moved further away from the hallowed vaults of the imposing village church. But they kept on walking. Anna could not afford even as much as had been provided by these families of more modest means. Pa would be buried in a quiet corner, along with many other men who died penniless in recent weeks, with no grave marker of any kind. He would be forgotten by the world.

With a grimace, she thought about the debts her father had left behind. Some she would be able to forget, as they were many years old and it would be unlikely that she would ever see those of her father's creditors again. Many would simply acknowledge that her father could no longer pay and so would consider the debts null and void. But there were too many that would expect her to make good on them, despite knowing she hadn't a sous to her name. Anna had no idea how she would ever make payment of such vast sums, and she feared that she would be followed wherever she might go by some very unsavory characters.

The gravediggers made their way through the churchyard to a boggy corner that was the furthest from the church that was possible and lowered the coffin into the gaping hole in the ground. Inside the hole, Anna could see a number of other rough coffins and even a couple of bodies wrapped in nothing more than a sheet of rough cloth. It made her sad to think that so many men and women ended their days in such a manner, cheek by jowl with people they had not even known. She wondered briefly if like Pa, they deserved such an ignominious end, or if they had been the unfortunate victims of poverty and sickness. She could only hope that what the bible taught was true, that man's earthly remains mattered little—that it was the soul that God cared about. Even for Pa, she prayed that he had done enough good in his life, somewhere, and had repented of his many sins so he might be permitted to enter heaven's gates.

The vicar sprinkled holy water over the grave, said a brief prayer of committal, and it was over. The gravediggers began to shovel the earth piled up beside the grave back into the hole, and the vicar made his way back inside the church—once Anna had handed him a small purse with all the coin she had left in the world. She'd had to sell Pa's wagon and everything in it just to give him this meager funeral. Even men of God needed to be paid their share.

Anna stood at the graveside and watched until the last shovelful of earth was back where it had come from and the gravediggers had moved away. "You got what you deserved," she said bitterly, remembering the beatings she'd gotten over the years. Pa had always been handy with his fists when in his cups, and he had been a sore loser. Anna had always been to blame for everything that had gone wrong in Pa's life, from saddling him with her very presence, to the times when a horse trade fell through because she'd fallen off the half-wild mounts he insisted on selling before they were ready. "But you were all I had, and so I am glad I have done right by you. Rest easy in your grave, Pa."

She walked away, her head held high. Anna had learned early that she needed to hide her feelings and to pretend to be that which she was not. Pa made her play so many roles as part of his many schemes and she'd learned young how to mimic those around her. Now, perhaps those skills would help her to move on and to find a better life. Anna knew that she could speak more eloquently than most of her kind, and she moved with grace. She was sure that she would be able to find a position in a fine house somewhere – even if she had to start at the bottom as a scullery maid or kitchen hand. Anna knew how to work hard – even if Pa never had.

She made her way back to the grand porch of the church and picked up the old carpetbag she had left there. Inside its battered, capacious exterior was everything Anna possessed. A tattered gown and clean undergarments, an old necklace Pa swore had belonged to her mother and a book of poetry she'd found in amongst her mother's old things some years earlier. Anna could barely read them, though she tried hard to do so. She could vaguely remember her mother reading them to her, but the recollection was so hazy and vague Anna often wondered if she'd simply imagined it.

Anna felt that she had known no other life than the one she had shared with Pa, though she knew that things had been very different whilst her mother had been alive. In her memories, Ma was always so much more refined than Pa, she had interests and skills that he had grown to be envious of, sparking his temper and spite. Anna often wondered how differently her life might have been had Ma lived longer. Perhaps she'd be able to read and write, have taken up a place in service and be respectable.

Instead, a life of trading in half-wild horses, card-sharping, and moving from town to town before anyone could catch Pa and demand he repay them had not given Anna many usable skills, other than the ability to act to deceive. She did not wish to continue in the vein that he had followed. His passing was her chance to make a new life, one where she could do good rather than harm. Yet there were few employers that would take on an unskilled, uneducated, and penniless woman such as herself. She'd probably end up having to throw herself on the mercy of the parish, though she vowed to do all she could to avoid such an outcome.

With a last glance at the church, bedecked with greenery for the Christmas celebrations, Anna turned and made her way out onto the street. As she passed through the lychgate, she vowed never to look back. There must be a way that she could turn her life around. There had to be someone or somewhere that she could go where she would not only be welcomed, but she would be useful and could make enough money to support herself. But it would not be here, not in this miserable little village where the chain that bound her had finally been buried.

Feeling more than a little trepidatious, Anna turned left out of the gate, putting Sparsholt behind her, and began to walk along the rutted road that would lead her first to Winchester and then onwards towards Farnham and Guildford. She prayed that there would be some work for her in one of these places, but if there were not, then she would continue onwards towards London. It was the wrong time of year to be searching for work; employers were often too caught up with arranging their Christmas celebrations for family and friends to be doing much business, but she had no choice.

A glimmer of blue began to appear between the clouds in the sky above as she walked briskly along the road to Winchester. Anna couldn't help but feel optimistic as the day progressed and the sun finally appeared, bathing her face in its light and gentle winter warmth. The death of her father would have made her sad, had he been the kind of father one actually mourned. With him gone, Anna now had the opportunity to create her own life in the way she wished. It would be hard work, and she knew that she would need a lot of luck, too—yet she knew, deep within, that life would get better for her.

As the miles passed, and the sun disappeared behind

ominous gray clouds once more, Anna's pace slowed, and her optimism faded. Her feet were riddled with blisters, her shoulders and arms ached from carrying her bag—even though she had shifted it from one hand to the other every half a mile or so—and she was bone-tired. She couldn't see so much as a shack anywhere along the road, and it was nearing nightfall. Anna began to fear that she might not find a safe place to stay for the night, so she tried unsuccessfully to pick up her pace once more. The pain in her sore feet was excruciating. "Ow," she moaned aloud. "What possessed me to think this was ever a good idea?"

Turning to look behind her, hopeful that she might see a carriage, or even a cart heading her way, Anna sighed heavily. There had been no passing traffic on the road all day, in either direction, and she could see no movement on the horizon now. She trudged on as the light grew dimmer, her pride and will sapped from the long day's walk and the prospect of a night alone by the roadside with nothing to keep her warm or fill her belly. She stopped by the side of the road and perched on a milestone that told her she only had another three miles until she reached Winchester. She could be there in two hours, maybe even less than that if she could forget how much her feet hurt and walk faster. It would be after dark, but at least she would be surrounded by houses and inns. Someone would surely be kind enough to take her in if she offered her services, cooking and cleaning, in return for a bed?

Wearily, she stood up, stretched, fidgeted her feet a little in her boots, grimacing at the discomfort, and then set off once more. Her progress was slow, and she winced with every step, but she kept pushing on. "I'll be there in no time," she repeated to herself over and over again—wishing with her every breath that it was true. She couldn't have traveled more than another half a mile when there was, finally, the sound of hooves and wheels coming along the road behind her.

Anna stopped and turned around. A large black shape was hurtling along the road, rocking and swaying as it fairly flew over the potholes and ruts in the road. The driver on the box was clad all in black, and he was whipping up his team of two with loud cries and rapid cracks of his whip. He didn't look to have seen her, so Anna stepped into the road a little and waved her hands wildly, praying he would stop and take her into Winchester. But as the carriage approached, Anna could see that he had no intention of stopping. The driver did not quit urging his horses onwards, and the phaeton approached her at a reckless speed.

Anna tried to step back out of the way, but her left heel caught in her skirts. Normally, she would have been more than capable of coping with such a mishap, but she was so weary that her balance seemed to have deserted her and she fell, tumbling into a ditch by the side of the road. She fell heavily onto the knee of the leg that was caught up in her skirt, and she heard a sickening crack as her body finally came to rest. She clutched at her leg and moaned. The pain was excruciating, and she tried to get up. She sobbed, though no tears fell onto her cheeks. It was as if her body was too tired even to do that.

Nobody would ever find her here; she hadn't seen the

ditch from the road herself, so she couldn't expect anyone else passing to see it—to see her. If she could at least get back onto the road, somebody might pass by. All she had left was hope, and there was precious little of that available to her—but she must do all she could to at least try to be seen, to be rescued. She pushed herself up on her weary arms and tried to grab hold of some of the wet grass on the bank to pull herself to her feet, but before she'd even tried to put weight on her bad leg, she collapsed back to the ground with a piercing scream.

"How am I ever to get out of here?" she moaned as she cradled her leg once again, and the tears finally began to fall. "I could die here. I must not be so weak. If I have to drag myself out of this dratted ditch, then that is what I must do." Taking a deep breath, she began to claw her way up the bank. The aches in her arms, her shoulders, and her back had been bothering her all day, but they had been nothing to the ferocious burning in her muscles now. Anna gritted her teeth, growling and screaming as she needed to, in order to get herself back onto the road. She was breathless and spent when she finally made it. Her head dropped to her chest, her lungs burning with the exertion, her body paralyzed by the pain that seemed to have taken over every part of her. She had done what she could. It would be up to God and the Fates to decide if it were enough.

CHAPTER TWO

"She threw a glass of wine in my face and told me, quite rightly, that she never wished to see me again," Edward, Lord Westerham said with a grin, leaning back against the plushly upholstered seats in his godmother's luxurious landau as they made their way to Winchester for Sunday Mass. His audience reacted as they so often did when he recanted the tales of his misdeeds. His father, opposite, smirked with suppressed amusement; his mother, sat beside her husband, gave him a look of exasperation; and his godmother sat beside him, gave a resoundingly contagious belly laugh. He laughed with her as she patted his hand fondly. She always loved the stories of his exploits in London.

"Dear Edward, I sometimes wonder if we shall ever see you happily wed," Lady Frances, Countess Tremaine said, tucking an arm through his and winking at him. He knew she did not mind if he ever settled down, as long as he was happy.

Lady Tremaine was what most people would call a character, Edward supposed. She was that unusual thing, a Countess in her own right, due to a favor her great-grandmother had done for the Crown. The entail upon the lands and title she had inherited conveyed all possession upon the firstborn of her family line, whatever their sex, and could never be taken from her by a husband upon marriage – nor could they have been taken from a firstborn daughter of hers, had she been blessed to have one.

Eccentric, clever as anyone he'd ever met, and always quick to think and act, Lady Frances did not care much for convention. She eschewed popular opinion and fashion, doing what she wished when she wished. Edward adored her, especially because she certainly didn't seem to mind that he showed little evidence of settling down—unlike his mother, Lady Frances' oldest and dearest friend.

The two women had grown up together and had been firm friends for as long as they could remember. They had learned to ride together, to embroider and all of the other ladylike arts—though to hear them tell it, Mama had often undertaken such tasks for Lady Tremaine so that she might bury her head in the books from her father's library. Edward had never met two people so very different, from their habits and interests to their physical appearance. It often made him wonder how their friendship had lasted so long.

Mama was tall and thin, with a very patrician manner. Societal mores were important to her, and

Edward doubted if she had ever set a foot out of line in her forty-nine years. She was a perfect lady, from her elegant posture to her dainty manners. She drew and painted beautiful watercolors, played the pianoforte with adequate skill and feeling, and sang like a lark. She never argued with Edward's father or anyone else for that matter. She was docile and did as she was expected, was the perfect hostess, and was never late to anything.

In stark contrast, Lady Frances was short and plump. She lived life on her terms. She drank port and smoked cigars—often refusing to leave the dinner table after supper in order to remain with the men and discuss politics and economics rather than retire to the drawing-room along with the other women. She talked knowledgeably about running her estates, the country's affairs, and could drink as heartily as any man. She was argumentative and stubborn—usually because she was so often right. She eschewed the ladylike arts, preferring to focus on what was going on in the world around her. She ran her home the way she pleased, and heaven help any man who tried to tell her otherwise. And, to her mind, punctuality was something that only ever applied to other people. Edward adored her.

Mama pursed her lips. "I do wish you would learn to be a little more circumspect, Edward," she said. "You are getting quite the reputation for being a flirt."

"Oh, Mama, do speak plainly," Edward said with a grin, knowing that she would never say what she truly thought of his behavior. "I am rapidly heading towards being known as a bounder and a cad."

"I did not say that, Edward," Mama said with a frown. "Nor would I ever say such a thing. I hope that no child of mine would ever be even considered to be such a thing. Why can you not see that people even implying them is most detrimental to your good character?"

"Simply because it is not true," Edward assured her. "I cannot be responsible for the ways other people might think of me, nor do I wish to be, Mama. I may possibly have let Lady Allingham think I cared more for her than I did, but I did not entirely deserve to have wine thrown in my face. I was a gentleman at all times. I cannot be held responsible for that silly ninny's thinking I was about to propose marriage simply because I was kind enough to dance with her once and take her to supper at Almack's."

"He's quite right, Harriet," Papa said, looking up briefly from his newspaper. "The boy cannot be expected to know the intentions of every filly that he dances with, nor should he try. Young girls these days, they all seem to think that every man must be after them just because they have a pretty face and a dowry. In my day, well, things were different."

"Of course they were, Harold," Lady Tremaine said, rolling her eyes. "Matches were made by our parents, as they should be. And nobody ever married for love, or attraction, or tried to wheedle their way out of a match made for them by their father. We accepted our fate and married whether we liked the person or not—and we made the very best of it we could." Her words were dripping with sarcasm. Edward had to try very hard to maintain a straight face. Papa hated to be wrong and hated it even more when it was Lady Tremaine making him feel small, though he often gave her such easy opportunities to do so.

"Now you are just being argumentative, Frances," Papa said. "You know full well what I meant. Decisions just weren't made on such silly nonsense as to how a girl felt when she danced with a chap."

"And it led to so many happy marriages," Lady Tremaine said with a dramatic swoon and a heavy sigh. She giggled, unable to maintain her composure. "Too many women, like myself, Harold, ended up wed to idiots because of the old ways. I'm not saying that things have improved any—but I do think that getting to know the man you are to wed and being sure you like him first isn't such a silly idea as you think."

"But things haven't really changed," Edward said thoughtfully. "Even though it appears that there is a choice, there really isn't for many young people today. They are pushed towards matches with people that are deemed suitable. They must have a title and wealth. They must dance well and look pretty. One's parents still have to approve a match or both men and women face being disinherited. It may appear that there is more choice, but I don't think there is."

Papa nodded his agreement. "And that is why every young girl is simply falling at Edward's feet because he is Lord Westerham, will one day become Earl of Winterton. He has a fine estate, will inherit an even better one, and has good standing in Society. He dresses well and is handsome—and has a fortune many would be envious of. He will inherit my seat in Parliament and is friends with Prinny. Any young woman in Society is going to be pushed—by her mother and father, no less—to ensnare him."

"I don't disagree," Mama said, now frowning at them all. "But I do think that because of that, Edward needs to be more circumspect in the manner in which he behaves. It does our family name no good to have him labeled as some bounder."

"Mama, I truly do not think that I will be," Edward assured her, reaching across the carriage to take her hand. "I am respectful, and I am polite. I flirt a little, but no more than any man should. I do not ever promise a girl anything I cannot or will not deliver. I cannot be held responsible for the silliness that they attach to those things in the privacy of their bedchambers. I can assure you that I have no intention of bringing the family name into disrepute." He lifted her hand to his lips and kissed her hand tenderly.

She sighed and reached out with her free hand to caress his cheek. "I do wish, sometimes, that you weren't so handsome or charming. It will be your undoing, my darling boy."

"I shall do my best to be sure it will not," Edward said solemnly, then leaned back in his seat once more.

Edward glanced out of the carriage as the conversation lulled. The carriage wasn't going very fast, as the driver was having to be extremely careful where he let the horses go. The weather in recent days had been wet and miserable. The roads were rutted, and the ditches and some of the fields on either side of the road were filled with water from the heavy rainfall overnight. It always surprised him to see what had once been green and verdant become a lake so swiftly. The flooding made the land exceptionally fertile, but it made choosing the right crops for such land more challenging for the men who made their living from it.

They passed a couple of men trudging by the side of the road, pickaxes, and shovels in hand. They were clearly trying to unblock the channels that allowed the water to drain from the road into the ditches and then onwards into the streams and rivers. Their faces were streaked with mud, their clothes sodden. Edward couldn't help feeling grateful that he was warm and dry inside the coach rather than out there in the inclement weather having to work so hard.

As they neared Winchester, there were more people on the roads, some clad in their Sunday best, others dressed for work as if it were any other day. All of them seemed to be ignoring what seemed to be a large pile of old clothes that had been left by the wayside. Edward stared at them wondering why anyone would have done such a thing. Something twitched, making the bundle move ever so slightly. Edward blinked and rubbed at his eyes, sure he must have been imagining it. The rain was coming down quite heavily again, the sound of the raindrops a cascade on the roof of the coach. The view through the carriage window was a little blurred. But when he looked back, Edward was certain that the bundle had moved again.

Perhaps it was just a rat, or something of that ilk, rummaging around to see if there was anything it might eat or that it might make use of for its nest, but Edward wasn't so sure. He banged his silver-topped cane on the roof of the carriage to tell the driver to stop. "Edward?" his mother asked, clearly surprised that he should do such a thing when they hadn't yet reached the church.

"I think there might be someone out there, by the side of the road," Edward said as the carriage came to a halt and he jumped out of the door.

He hurried to where the bundle lay. As he drew closer, it was quite clear that it was a person, though their leg was poking out at a most peculiar angle. He wondered why nobody else had seemed even to see it. Those on foot were just walking by, shielding their faces from the rain. He supposed they were only in a hurry to get out of the cold and wet weather, so had little time to look around them, but it seemed strange to him that they could walk by someone in need.

Kneeling beside the body, the mud soaked through Edward's breeches. It was cold as ice and chilled him to the bone. Edward shuddered. To have met your end in such a way, in the mud, alone, was simply horrific to his mind. Edward rolled the body over and gasped.

The face that looked up at him was that of a young woman, her hair and clothes utterly caked in mud. Her skin, between the brown streaks, was as pale as milk. She was cold as ice, and her body was stiff and unyielding, as though she were dead, but Edward could see a tiny rise and fall in her chest. "It's a young woman. She's badly hurt—but she's alive," he cried out as his father clambered out of the carriage and made his way towards him.

Lady Tremaine poked her head out of the door. "Bring her inside. I think we can miss church this once.

We shall take her home and fetch Doctor Winston immediately."

Edward and his father lifted the young woman. She was light as a feather. Edward shook his head at his father, then stared angrily at the people who had just walked by this poor creature. "How can anyone do that?" he asked.

"They don't see," his father said, his face saddened by it. "And often, they don't have enough to feed their own families, much less offer charity to anyone else. They probably thought she was already dead. I'm afraid they see death more often than our kind do—they're used to it."

Such a truth seemed too hard to bear, but it appeared that it was indeed so. Nobody even queried them while they were picking up the body and taking it away. He and his father could have had all manner of dastardly intentions towards this half-dead creature, yet there was nobody who would speak for her. It was a sad indictment on the world they lived in, Edward thought.

He and his father heaved the young woman onto the floor of the carriage out of the wind and rain. Lady Tremaine had laid a large blanket on the seat behind the driver, and she nodded that Edward should lift the body onto it. He did so, and Lady Tremaine then covered the girl with another blanket. "We shall have to sit tight," she said with a smile as Papa clambered into the coach and took his seat by the window once more. Mama moved up close to him, her nose wrinkling a little as she did so as she tried with no luck to avoid the mud that was now covering his coat and boots. Lady Tremaine sat next to her and patted the tiny patch of the bench left beside her, indicating that Edward should take it.

"I can sit on the floor," he said. "I'm filthy all over— not just my boots. And, I think it wise that someone make sure our patient does not fall and do herself any greater damage."

CHAPTER THREE

The world seemed to be covered with a veil when Anna next opened her eyes. Everything around her was clean and bright but blurry and indistinct. The walls of the room she found herself in were whitewashed, the linens on the bed pristine. The bed was soft and warm, and she seemed to be clad in a clean cotton shift, but the details were hard to make out. The sun was shining through a small window just below the beams of the roof that sloped slightly over the head of the bed. There seemed to be sturdy pieces of fine wooden furniture against the walls, and a washstand set in the corner by the door.

Anna could only think that she must be dreaming because she had never woken in a chamber such as this in all her life. Her throat was raw, there was sleep in her eyes, and her nose felt stuffy. There was a pounding behind her eyes, and her head felt as though it was being pressed in a vice. Her body was stiff and sore, and there was a great deal of pain in her left leg. Anna tried to sit up but found her body was so weak that she could barely lift her head. She closed her eyes and sank back onto the pillow.

She must have slept for some time, for the next time she awoke, the drapes had been pulled, and the room was now lit by a lamp held by a neatly attired maid, clad in a plain black gown and a white apron and cap, leaning over the bed to peer into her face. "I think she's coming around," the young woman said in a thick West Country burr. The sound of it made Anna feel happy and sad all at once. The maid's voice and her words reminded Anna of the way her mother had spoken.

Anna tried to open her eyes wider and to speak, but her throat was so sore that she could manage little more than a croak. "Don't try to speak," the maid said, reaching out and placing a tender hand upon Anna's arm. She turned towards the door where Anna could now see another figure was standing. This woman was older. She had iron-gray hair and wore an old-fashioned black gown with a large ring, filled with keys, hanging at her waist.

"I'll fetch Lady Tremaine. She'll be glad to know our guest is finally on the mend," the older woman said and disappeared.

"That's Mrs. Cartwright," the maid said as she put down the lamp and picked up a glass of water. "Would you like some?" Anna tried to nod. The maid held the glass to Anna's lips. The water was cool and soothed the scratchiness in her throat a little. Anna tried again to speak but only ended up coughing loudly. "There, now, don't try so hard," the maid said, setting down the glass of water and putting a steadying hand on Anna's shoulder.

Anna leaned back, letting the pillow beneath her take the full weight of her heavy head. The maid went to the washstand where she poured water into the bowl and brought it towards the bed. "Mrs. Trimble's the housekeeper," the maid explained. "She'll be back shortly, bringing her Ladyship, so we'd best give you a lick." She took a cloth from inside the bowl and squeezed out the excess water from it before she then ran it over Anna's face.

The cloth was cooling and soothing, and Anna sighed as the maid went about her task of making sure Anna looked presentable enough for her employer. A swift, but thorough washing was undertaken, Anna's hair was combed and then plaited, and the maid helped Anna to sit up a little, propping her up with a couple of extra pillows she pulled out from the trunk at the end of the bed. "There, you look a lot brighter now," the girl said with a gentle smile as she gathered the jug and bowl together and moved towards the door. "I'll be back later with some soup. Don't worry; you'll be quite alright."

Anna tried to smile, but her face felt tight and sore. She wondered just how badly she had been hurt and how unwell she must have been not to have remembered even being brought here to this place. She couldn't help feeling a little nervous at meeting her Ladyship. Mrs. Cartwright had seemed quite daunting enough to a girl like Anna, who was used to traveling from town to town, rarely ever sleeping under a roof—let alone one suitable for a peer of the realm.

Thankfully, she did not have very long to wait before she found out exactly the kind of woman that her Ladyship might be. She appeared in the doorway just moments later. She was short and round and had a beaming smile that put Anna at her ease immediately. Mrs. Cartwright stood behind her. Her Ladyship approached the bed. Mrs. Cartwright moved a chair closer so her employer might sit beside Anna.

"Well, my dear, you've had a difficult time, haven't you," her Ladyship said reaching out and patting Anna's hand kindly. "Now, I am glad to see you awake, so we might now be more formally introduced. I am Lady Frances Tremaine, and you are my guest, until you are quite well, here at Trelawney Hall."

"Thank you," Anna croaked awkwardly. She gulped a little, trying to get some moisture back into her mouth and throat, then cleared her throat as best she could. "That is most generous of you. I am honored to meet you, your Ladyship," she continued, her voice wavering, pitching high and low, sounding scratchy and awkward— with nerves as well as from lack of use. "I'm Anna Campbell."

"I am very pleased to meet you." Lady Tremaine gave Anna's hand a squeeze and smiled at her again. Anna was taken aback by the lady's friendly manner. She was the daughter of a card sharp and gambler. To be treated almost as an equal was quite unexpected.

"Your Ladyship, I don't remember how I got here," she confessed.

"I am not surprised by that at all, my dear. We thought you were dead when we first found you. My godson spotted you by the side of the road."

"I am very grateful for it," Anna said fervently, her

voice cracking with the emotion and the continuing pain she still felt. "I shall pay you back every penny you've spent upon me, I swear it."

"My dear girl, there is no need for such promises. We were glad to help you. It is the Christian thing to do. But, if you don't mind my asking, how did you come to be half-in and half-out of that ditch in the first instance?"

Anna thought about that for a moment. Everything was hazy in her memory, but it slowly began to swim back into focus. "I was walking along the road on Saturday night. I'd buried my father earlier in the day, and I wanted to get to Winchester so I could find somewhere to sleep for the night. I had paused, just for a moment, and this carriage came out of nowhere. He was racing so fast. It was one of those phaetons, I think, and there were two horses in the shafts. I've never seen anything go that quick."

"And the carriage knocked you down?" Lady Tremaine pressed gently.

"It did. One moment I was on the road, watching it come at me, and the next I was in the ditch."

"And that was how you broke your leg?"

"Ah, that," Anna said with a bitter chuckle. "I caught my heel in my dress. I lost my balance, and over I went, my foot still hoicked up. I think I'll remember the sound of it cracking as long as I live."

"But you managed to drag yourself back onto the road?"

"I did, but it took everything I had to do so," Anna admitted. "I remember lying there for some time; it grew dark and it got colder and colder and then I don't remember anything else."

Lady Tremaine nodded. "You have had a dreadful ordeal. But you are safe now, and I think I can tell you of at least some of what has occurred since." Anna gave her an encouraging look. She needed to know everything she could. "As I said, we found you by the road on Sunday morning. We were on our way to church. My godson, Edward, spotted you from quite a way away and insisted we stop. He and his father brought you into the carriage, and we brought you here. You were so cold and were barely breathing."

"I am sorry to have been such trouble," Anna said honestly. She never liked to be a burden to anyone.

"Oh, you have been no trouble at all," Lady Tremaine reassured her. "Has she, Mrs. Trimble?"

"Not a bit of it," the housekeeper said nicely enough, but Anna could tell that she had probably been far more bother to the staff of this fine house than they would ever tell their kindly employer.

"Well, I am grateful for all of your assistance," Anna said. "I shall never be able to repay you, but I could work off my debt, once I am fully able to, of course." She nodded to her leg and smiled wanly.

"That isn't necessary," Lady Tremaine said dismissively. She looked Anna in the eye as if she were looking deep into her soul. It was disconcerting, but it seemed that the older woman found what she was looking for as she smiled reassuringly before she continued her tale. "Anyway, we brought you here, and dear Dr Winston set your leg and gave us some salve for your bruises. He thought you'd probably gotten pneumonia and that because of the pain and the cold, you'd not wake for a few days."

"How long was I unconscious?" Anna asked.

"Almost two weeks," Mrs. Cartwright said. "But now you're back with us, I'm sure it won't be long before you're back on your feet, itching for something to do."

The housekeeper's prediction turned out to be most accurate. It didn't take Anna long to be fed up with being trapped in her bed. She was soon up and about, using a cane to support her weight as she hobbled around the many corridors of Trelawney Hall. She made her way down to the kitchens every day and helped Cook with preparing the vegetables, the chambermaids with cleaning the brasses, and whatever else she could do whilst seated. She knew her place and had no intention of being accused of taking advantage of Lady Tremaine's generosity.

As for her ladyship, she insisted upon seeing Anna every day. She wanted to know how Anna was progressing in her recovery, and it seemed that she truly enjoyed Anna's company. Anna couldn't help but admire the feisty older lady. It seemed to Anna that she lived life on her own terms—something few women were permitted to do in their world. Her Ladyship didn't give a fig for anyone's opinion but her own, she ran her estates the way she saw fit—eschewing more modern practices that increased yield for the landowner in favor of methods that had been used for centuries and benefitted the land and all the people that lived on it.

Anna was never treated like a servant, and it

surprised her that none of the household servants were either. Each was treated with kindness and warmth. Lady Tremaine knew every one of their names, from Mrs. Cartwright and Harker, the butler, down to the kitchen boy, Arthur, and the stable lad, Will. She was generous. Anna didn't hear a single grumble about low wages or anyone being expected to do more than their fair share of work. They all had Sunday off and a half-day in the week—but if they wanted it, Lady Tremaine never refused them taking a whole day. Because she was so good, nobody ever took more time than they needed, and so the house ran smoothly.

But from all she had heard, everything in the house always changed when Lord William Comey blew in like a whirlwind to visit his great aunt. The staff regaled her with tales of his arrogance and rudeness at supper time around the large kitchen table. He liked fast carriages, faster horses, and spent much of his time in London, ensconced in one or other of the gentleman's clubs there, gambling his quarterly allowance away. He only came to visit when he needed an advance on his next quarter's funds from what Mrs. Trimble said—and everyone felt that Lady Tremaine was too kind to him, as she always agreed to give him the money he asked for.

As Anna got up the one morning before Christmas Eve and stretched, she pushed herself up onto her feet and hobbled across the chamber so she might look out her window. It looked down over the drive, where she saw a phaeton approaching and sighed. Not only did the sporty carriage remind her again of the ordeal that had brought her here to Trelawney Hall, but it also heralded two or three days of misery for everyone in the household if the tales she had heard were to be believed. Anna shivered a little. She had little doubt that the driver on the box would turn out to be Lady Tremaine's wayward great-nephew, Viscount William Comey.

She dressed quickly and made her way downstairs, hobbling as quickly as she could muster, taking one step at a time. Dr Winston had assured her that she would have to remain in her splints for at least two months more, and she was trying to be patient—but she was rapidly learning that it was not one of her virtues. She was determined to give her benefactress warning of what was hurtling up the driveway towards them.

As far as Anna knew, Viscount Comey had not informed anyone that he would be joining them for Christmas, though it would have been surprising if he had not done so. Lady Tremaine hosted one of the most talked-about balls in the county on Christmas Eve night. Everyone in Society would be there. She doubted if Viscount Comey cared much about being with his family at Christmas, but he did care about his position amongst the *ton*. She hurried into the breakfast room. Lady Tremaine was sat at the table, eating toast and sipping at her hot chocolate, humming a little tune.

"He's here," Anna said breathlessly, hanging on to the door frame, puffing a little from her exertions. "Viscount Comey's here."

"Drat," Lady Tremaine said, throwing down her napkin onto the table and rising from her chair. "I shall have to be nice to him, I suppose." Her obvious annoyance amused Anna. She'd never known anyone to be so honest about disliking their relatives before.

Lady Tremaine walked to the doorway where Anna was still trying to catch her breath and helped Anna to a seat before going out into the hallway. "Harker," Lady Tremaine called out.

The butler appeared as if he'd just been hidden around the corner and bowed politely to his mistress. "Your Ladyship?"

"My great-nephew is here, again," she said, raising her eyebrows to show her exasperation. "Please, can you have Mrs. Trimble make up the Blue Room for him and fetch a fresh pot of coffee? He's bound to want it hot and strong, so let us be ready."

Harker vanished and Lady Tremaine moved to sit by Anna's side. "You don't need to stay if you do not want to. Nobody would blame you if you chose to hide away in your rooms. When he last came, you were still unconscious—you may come to be very grateful for that."

Anna had never heard Lady Tremaine be so dismissive of anyone. She always managed to find a kind word or an admirable feature in the most unpleasant of people. That she was echoing the disdain Anna had found below stairs for this man meant he must be truly odious. "I think I am brave enough to face it," Anna said with a wry grin. As far as she was concerned, nobody could be worse than her father.

CHAPTER FOUR

"Dearest Aunt," Viscount Comey said, swooping into the hallway like an oversized bat, his black cape billowing out behind him in dramatic fashion, revealing a maroon velvet waistcoat embroidered with gold thread and tiny seed pearls, and an emerald green cravat with a diamond pin. He was tall, with dark hair that he wore slicked back into a thin little ponytail, tied with a ribbon that matched his waistcoat perfectly. His face was narrow, his chin pointed, giving him a slightly weaselly appearance. His hairline was receding, making his forehead seem too wide and too high, while his nose was as long and straight as his lips were thin.

He bowed perfunctorily, then leaned down to kiss the air above his great-aunt's cheeks. Anna watched the exchange between her benefactress and her great-nephew through the open door of the breakfast room, surprised by Lady Tremaine's brittle posture and obvious discomfort in the man's presence. She had never before seemed to be affected by anyone in such a manner as far as Anna had seen. "William, what a surprise," Lady Tremaine said, her tone disdainful as if she did not quite dare to chastise him for his lack of manners in simply turning up without having announced his intentions to visit. "We weren't expecting you. I presume you intend to stay through Christmas?"

"I should be honored, if it is not too much trouble, Aunt Frances?" Viscount Comey said, his expression and voice both oozing with false charm. "I shall leave before the New Year, though, as I have business to attend to in London."

"Of course, it would be no trouble," Lady Tremaine said through slightly gritted teeth. It surprised Anna to see her being so polite and even deferential. Anna liked how blunt Lady Tremaine could be with those she thought to be fools, or that she disliked. From what Anna had heard, Lady Tremaine not only thought her great-nephew to be quite devoid of any intelligence, and also disliked him intensely. It made Anna wonder why. Then she realized that it was probably just because her Lady-ship had been caught off guard.

"I shall have your usual rooms made up for you, William," Lady Tremaine said in a cool voice that seemed much more in character. "You can amuse yourself in the library until they are ready. Please don't bother the servants too much. There is much to do before tonight's ball."

"Of course not, Aunt. I shall be quiet as a mouse. They shall not hear a peep from me all afternoon. Though I would be most grateful if you could have Harker take my things up and to have them unpacked and pressed, and perhaps something to eat would be lovely, if it is no trouble?"

Lady Frances nodded and watched as her nephew made his way towards the library. Anna was sure she saw an expression of disgust pass over the older lady's face, but she schooled her features again so quickly that Anna could not be entirely sure whether she had imagined it or not. Anna herself knew, instinctively, that she did not like Viscount Comey. She supposed Viscount Comey was good-looking enough, though he was too thin and too angular for her tastes. He certainly had a penchant for fine tailoring and bright colors underneath that black cloak of his. Viscount Comey was undoubtedly a peacock, and Anna suspected him of being a dandy, and possibly worse, but would never have dared to say such a thing—either to him or to Lady Tremaine.

But it was not his obvious vanity that had offended her so. Viscount Comey had seemed unabashed by his unannounced arrival and the extra work it would mean for his aunt's household—especially as he must have been aware that his aunt's annual Christmas ball was to take place this very evening. He was dismissive of his aunt's obvious disdain, and there was something shifty about the manner in which he behaved that made Anna instinctively dislike and distrust him. His eyes, so dark and close-set, reminded Anna of her father, constantly darting around him—always looking out for an opportunity to exploit. Viscount Comey may have a title and be the heir to Lady Tremaine's estates, but he was as much of a gambler on the make as Pa had been—Anna was sure of it.

Lady Tremaine came back into the breakfast room and sat down beside Anna. "Oh well," she said with a heavy sigh. "I had hoped that I might be able to enjoy Christmas this year."

"Is he truly so dreadful?" Anna asked cautiously. She still had not worked out what the boundaries were in her relationship with Lady Tremaine. She wasn't treated as a servant, though she did her best to help out as much as she could. Lady Tremaine, in some ways, treated her as a daughter—or perhaps a niece, always concerned about her welfare and dismissive of her wish to repay her hostess for all her kindnesses.

"Oh, no," Lady Tremaine said, her expression unusually hard as flint. "He's much worse. I truly wish that there was someone else that I could leave my estate to, but sadly my husband and I were never blessed with children, and he is the only one left alive from my dear sister's line. William will have it mortgaged to the hilt to pay for his gambling and his fancy clothes before I've been in my grave a twelvemonth. That boy will be the end of the Tremaine name, and our standing in the world —you mark my words."

"I am sorry," Anna said awkwardly, not knowing what else to say. She knew just how dreadful it was to live with a man that gambled everything he possessed away. She'd suffered many an empty belly, often accompanied by a drunken beating, because Pa hadn't known when to stop.

"If only I'd had a child of my own," Lady Tremaine mused, her expression softening. She seemed almost melancholy. "I'd have liked a daughter or a son."

Anna stayed silent. There truly was nothing she could say to that. She resisted the urge to reach out and cover Lady Tremaine's hand with her own, to let the older woman know that she understood and that she cared. It would not be proper for her to be so intimate with a woman so far above her socially, so she stayed quiet and hoped that Lady Tremaine knew that she cared.

The silence stretched out between them, but it was not uncomfortable. Anna was always surprised by just how easy it was to be with Lady Tremaine. She'd certainly never felt that way with an older woman before —much less with anyone of the nobility. Until now, she'd always been polite, had bobbed curtsies and waited until she was spoken to with such people. Mostly, they simply ignored her. Lady Tremaine was so very different in that respect.

Lady Tremaine sipped at her chocolate and indicated that Anna should help herself to food and drink. "Eat up; you need to build up your strength," she urged.

"I shall go down to the kitchen shortly," Anna said. She'd never dare to eat in this elegant room, opposite Lady Tremaine. She wouldn't know where to begin when it came to using the correct cutlery, let alone how to eat in a ladylike manner. Lady Tremaine would be aghast to see Anna eat, of that Anna was certain.

"My dear, I will not be offended if you eat in large bites and don't know the difference between a soup spoon and a dessert spoon," Lady Tremaine insisted. "I know you did not have the upbringing I did. But, if you are to stay on as my companion—and I do hope you will do so once you are well—you will need to begin to learn such things, and there is no better time for you to begin to learn than now."

Anna's mouth dropped open. "You wish me to stay? As your companion?" she asked, flabbergasted at such a suggestion.

"I do. I enjoy your company. You are polite and kind. You present yourself as well as you can, under the circumstances, and you are unfailingly amusing. You need a position. I should think it would suit us both very well indeed."

"I... I don't know what to say," Anna stuttered.

"Say yes, you silly girl," Lady Tremaine said, grinning.

"Yes," Anna echoed before giggling nervously for a moment. "I cannot thank you enough."

"You did say you would be happy to work your debts to me. It seems as feasible a manner for you to do so as any."

"But I am the daughter of a card sharp, a gambler—a horse trader," Anna said, still bewildered by the sudden turn of events. "What would everyone say?"

"What they might say is of little consequence to me, my dear. Oh, they may talk behind our backs, but there is one unfailingly silly thing about Society – they would never dare say such things to my face." She paused and smiled at Anna warmly. "Despite your upbringing, you are none of those things – it would do you well to remember that."

Lady Tremaine nodded towards the library. "My great-nephew is the son of a viscount, yet he is all of those things—and probably many that are much worse. He may have the polish and breeding of the aristocracy, but he has as much nobility and strength of character as your departed father."

Anna felt tears prick at the backs of her eyes, but she was determined not to shed them. She had not known such a feeling of belonging, of being wanted at any time in her short life. Lady Tremaine was offering her the world—and she would be a fool not to take it. Yet she feared for the way in which the older woman's decision might be construed amongst the *ton*. Lady Tremaine did not live as she was expected to as it was, for her to take such a woman as Anna into the homes of the aristocracy, to expect them to accept her as Lady Tremaine's companion, to have her sit at their dining tables and be part of their conversations, would be a huge risk.

"I want to say yes," she admitted. "But I cannot think that anyone will ever accept me as such."

"Piffle," Lady Tremaine said. "If they refuse to accept you, then they will be refusing to accept me. I won't deny you need a little polish before we present you in public, but I don't think it will take us long to have you ready to face whatever society might throw at you. I enjoy your company. I like your forthright manner. I enjoy your way of seeing things. As far as I am concerned, those attributes alone make you the perfect companion for me. I do not care one jot what society thinks of it, and you shouldn't, either." With that said, Lady Tremaine stood up, drank the final few drops of her chocolate, set down her cup, kissed the top of Anna's head, and left the room.

Anna sat there alone for a few minutes, replaying the

conversation she had just shared with Lady Tremaine. It seemed too good to possibly be true. She was not born to this world. She had no education to speak of, and no refinement at all—yet, this wonderful lady wished her, Anna Campbell, to be her companion. It was the sort of position that would only ever be offered to some genteel young lady, not a commoner like Anna. She'd find herself in the parlors and dining rooms of some of the finest homes in the county—maybe even all of England. She'd be taken to London and to Bath, where she would accompany Lady Tremaine to all manner of events, from balls and card parties to suppers and dances. It was the kind of life a young girl like her could only dream of—yet it was being offered to her, without question, without limits.

Anna stood up, looked around her, and wondered if she dared to stay and eat here in the breakfast room, as Lady Tremaine had suggested. The silver servers were full of delicious tidbits; she knew that as she'd often helped Cook to fill them each morning. But it did not yet feel real—and she did not think that she possessed the manners and habits needed to eat in such an elegant room.

"Aunt," Viscount Comey said, bursting into the room and into Anna's thoughts. "Oh, she is not here?" he asked Anna. "I don't know how she ever gets anything done in this ridiculous old place. I shall have it pulled down the moment she has passed and get rid of every member of this useless household."

His words made Anna bristle. It seemed to her that everything he did was done at speed. He had spoken at a rate of knots that Anna found hard to keep up with; from what she'd seen of his progress up the driveway, he drove and rode as fast as the wind—and it seemed that his intentions for Lady Tremaine's family home and everyone in it would be carried out as swiftly as he could manage once he had the power to do so. It was enough to make a girl wish she were anywhere other than here before him.

"She has gone to make the arrangements for your stay, and for this evening, of course, my Lord," Anna said, her tone brisk and icy cold.

Viscount Comey tilted his head to one side and studied her. His eyes roamed from the top of her head to the tips of Anna's toes. A flash of lust crossed his features, but it was not tempered by interest or warmth—the look was cold, calculating. It made Anna shudder. "You must be the chit she's been nursing," he said, his upper lip curling into a sneer. "Well, you'll do. Fetch me some fresh coffee and a blanket. The library is ice cold. Did my aunt know the fires have yet to be lit?"

Anna was sure that her Ladyship had most certainly known. But it would not do her any favors to anger him by telling him so. "I am sure it is simply an oversight. I can have one of the maids come up immediately," she said.

"Why can you not do it?" Viscount Comey asked. "I need warmth now, not in a quarter of an hour when one of my aunt's lazy household gets around to it. And why aren't you standing in the presence of your betters, you insolent creature?"

Anna stood up slowly and picked up her cane, anger bubbling up inside her at this man's rudeness and disdain for those he clearly saw as being beneath him. She leaned on the silver-topped ebony stick heavily and poked out her heavily splinted leg. "I shall be glad to help you, my Lord, by fetching someone who can assist you."

Anna didn't wait for him to say anything else; she simply hurried downstairs to the kitchens where most of the staff were seated around the large pine table eating their breakfast. Anna told Harker all that Viscount Comey had requested, and he disappeared to go and arrange everything promptly.

Anna took his now empty seat at the table to catch her breath and tried to calm herself once more. "He's a piece of work, isn't he?" Cook said as she laid a plate of bacon and eggs down in front of Anna.

"He is that," she agreed as she reached across the table and grabbed a slice of freshly baked bread, which she then slathered with butter that had been churned just yesterday. Anger had always made her hungry.

"He won't be here long," Mrs. Trimble said, putting a reassuring hand on Anna's shoulder as she got up to leave. "He never stays more than a few days."

"I shall have to try my best to stay out of his way," Anna said as she chewed on a mouthful of the delicious bread. "I do not know if I will be able to bite my tongue if he is so rude to me again."

These thoughts troubled Anna all day as she went about assisting the maids as they decorated the house and helped Cook prepare the fairings and fancies for the ball that night. If she accepted Lady Tremaine's generous offer, she would be forced to spend more time with the odious Viscount Comey—something she had no wish to do. But to turn down such generosity, such an opportunity to better herself would be churlish and would only hurt herself.

There would be much to learn if she were to become her Ladyship's companion. Anna wasn't sure if she would ever be able to do so. She'd never been particularly graceful, or patient. She'd need to learn to be both—and that was without all the little things, like being able to drink from a wine glass without leaving a mark or cutting food into tiny bites and chewing slowly and thoroughly before swallowing. She'd probably need to learn to read and write, and so much more. It would change her life. It would change her. She would never need to fear being hungry or cold ever again. But she might not be able to contain her disapproval of Lady Tremaine's dreadful great-nephew—and Anna did not ever wish to disappoint or embarrass Lady Tremaine by insulting her only family.

CHAPTER FIVE

Anna retired to her chamber after supper and watched the carriages as they began to arrive for the ball. She watched as their inhabitants climbed down, admiring their finery, mimicking the manner in which the ladies walked and held their hands and their heads. It all felt so fake and peculiar to her. She was certain that such behaviors would never become second nature to her as they were to them. It gave her yet another reason to say no to Lady Tremaine, though it was not a good enough reason not to at least try.

Wondering what it must feel like to be clad in such finery, and to be treated with such respect, Anna lay down upon her bed and stared up at the ceiling. She let her thoughts drift as she listened to the hubbub of happy people building in the hallway and ballroom below. Anna could make out the strains of a popular tune, played by the string quartet that Lady Tremaine had hired for the evening. It was jolly and bright. Anna wondered if people were dancing. She had always loved to dance, though she doubted that her steps would be considered in any way elegant enough for such a fine setting as Lady Tremaine's richly decorated ballroom.

Anna couldn't bear just lying there, not knowing what was happening below her. She had to see what would be expected of her if she were to take on the role of Lady Tremaine's companion, to experience the kinds of events she would be expected to attend and the ways in which she might be expected to behave. She jumped up and hobbled out of her room, down the back stairs, and snuck onto the minstrel's gallery above the ballroom. An elaborate wooden frieze at the front of the gallery shielded the musicians from sight of the people down below, and so she was able to move to the front and peer out at them through the lattice. The musicians grinned at her but continued to play.

Anna marveled at the richness of the ladies' gowns and the daintiness of their steps as they were whirled around the room by their handsomely clad partners. Lady Tremaine sat on a dais, surrounded by three other older women. She was talking most intently with a tall lady to her right. They seemed very intimate and laughed together often. Anna was glad to see her enjoying herself. Viscount Comey approached the dais and bowed obsequiously. Lady Tremaine merely nodded at him. There was no warmth in her gaze. Anna wasn't surprised that Lady Tremaine seemed to dislike her great-nephew as much as she did, but she was surprised that she didn't seem to mind if everybody knew it.

Viscount Comey backed away from the dais, still facing her, then turned abruptly, his face black as thunder, and marched towards a group of young women at the end of the ballroom. He offered his hand to one of them. She looked a little desperately to her companions, but they did not come to her aid, and so she was forced to take his hand and go out onto the dancefloor with him. Anna felt sorry for the poor girl, especially as Viscount Comey continued to look over at his aunt, his eyes narrowed, and lips pursed in his impotent rage at her dismissal of him in public.

But Anna's attention soon moved away from the unpleasant expressions of Viscount Comey, because as the musicians struck up the next reel, another young man approached the dais and bowed to Lady Tremaine and the woman next to her. This time, both women looked delighted to see him. Anna wondered who he was. He was tall, with broad shoulders and slim hips. His chestnut hair shone in the light of the candelabra overhead, and Anna noticed that a few wayward curls had escaped his neat ponytail, curling becomingly around his ears and falling onto his forehead. He had a smiling mouth and warm blue eyes. She knew such a man would never look at a girl like her, but she couldn't help imagining herself in his arms, being whisked around the floor, with those glorious eyes gazing down at her, filled with love.

EDWARD HAD ALWAYS ENJOYED CHRISTMAS, and he had always felt that the real festivities began at his godmother's Christmas Eve ball. Lady Frances looked positively joyful this evening, and Edward was pleased to see his mother enjoying herself just as much. As always, Trelawney Hall was filled with greenery from the nearby woodlands; holly boughs, mistletoe, and evergreens of all kinds were hanging from the ceilings, wound around banisters, and draped over mantels. Anyone who was anyone was there, dancing, playing cards, or just gossiping amongst themselves. Edward moved amongst them, smiling and greeting the people he knew and liked, nodding politely to those he was not so keen on.

"Westerham!" A loud booming voice hailed him from across the ballroom. Edward grinned. He'd not expected Prinny to make it to Lady Frances' ball this year. As the Prince Regent, he had so many demands upon his time now, and Edward had expected him to remain in London for the festive season.

"Your Highness," Edward said as he approached the voluminous figure of his dear friend. He bowed, but Prinny raised him and embraced him.

"Westerham, your dear godmother has outdone herself—yet again," he said gesturing around them. "How does she do it? I wish I knew. Nobody ever turns her down, do they?"

"No, I don't think they do," Edward agreed. "I think they come to see if she has become even more eccentric since last year."

"You are probably right," Prinny chortled. "There is nobody like her in all the kingdom."

"Will you be staying with us throughout Christmas? I

am sure Lady Frances' will have the royal suite ready for you."

"No, I have only stopped in as a courtesy. I move onwards to London immediately," Prinny said nonchalantly. "This evening shall be my Christmas this year."

Edward felt for his old friend. To be stuck in a coach, traveling the length and breadth of the country at Christmastime, seemed particularly harsh, though Prinny was sure to get a warm welcome at any estate he stopped at along the way. He would not go without good company, fine wine, and excellent festive fare unless he chose to. "You could not have chosen a finer place to stop and rest."

"Indeed, and now I am going in search of your godmother's famous port stores and hope to coax the lovely Cook to make me some of her delightful pheasant pies to keep me company upon my journey. Do you think either of them will deny me my little pleasures?"

"I think they will both be honored to oblige you, Your Highness."

Prinny waddled off, and Edward glanced around the room at the smiling faces surrounding him. He would usually be on the dancefloor for much of the night, yet for some unknown reason, he simply did not feel like dancing tonight. He longed for some peace and quiet, so he made his way out of the crowded ballroom, across the hallway, and up the stairs.

He turned to walk along the long gallery. This wide corridor-like room had always been one of his favorite places to be in Trelawney Hall. On the walls, endless paintings of Lady Frances' ancestors peered down at him, while glass-doored cabinets displayed all manner of peculiar items that members of the family had collected over the years. Edward's favorite item had always been the elaborate music box that Lady Frances' father had brought back from Europe following his Grand Tour. It was as tall as Edward, an exact replica of Trelawney House, and its clever mechanism played a Pleyel sonatina. He wound the key and watched as the little figures moved around the grand house in time to the tinkling bells and smiled.

"It is such a lovely tune, isn't it, my Lord?" a soft voice asked from just behind him. Edward hadn't noticed anyone following him upstairs, and he had obviously been utterly lost in the moment not to hear them approaching him. He turned to see a young woman in a plain gray gown stood before him. She looked a little familiar, though he couldn't quite place her.

This young lady wasn't dressed for the ball. Her hair was pinned in quite a plain bun at the back of her head with no additional braiding or curls, as the girls downstairs were wearing, though he could see that it was a striking shade of auburn. Her eyes were her most compelling feature. Green, with a slight slant to them that reminded him of a cat. Her skin was pale, creamy with pink flushes at her cheeks and a smattering of freckles over her nose. She was quite lovely.

"It has always been my favorite piece," Edward admitted. "Excuse me, you'll think me very rude, but have we met?"

"I don't think so," the young woman said with a shy smile, bobbing him a pretty, though slightly off-balance curtsey. "And I am being dreadfully rude approaching you and speaking to you like this. Please forgive me, my Lord. I'm just a guest in this house whilst I recuperate from an accident."

"Oh, my," Edward gasped, noticing that she was carrying a cane, though her bad leg was hidden by her skirts. "You're the young woman we found by the roadside. My godmother said you were feeling much better. Why aren't you downstairs enjoying the ball?"

"I'm not the kind of girl that gets to go to such events, my Lord," she said honestly. "And I shouldn't be here talking to you, either, so if you'll forgive me, I'll be on my way."

"Nonsense. I am free to talk to whomever I please, and right now, that is you, Miss Campbell. It is Miss Campbell, is it not?"

"It is," she said. "Anna is enough, though. I'm no parlor miss."

"Edward, Lord Westerham, at your service." He bowed deeply.

"I saw you arrive," Miss Campbell admitted. "Watched you speak with Lady Tremaine and a lady sat beside her."

"That was probably my mother, Lady Winterton. They are fast friends."

"I am glad for her Ladyship that she seemed to be enjoying herself so greatly. She's been so very kind to me."

"She's kind to everyone. I've never known anyone with a heart quite so open to everyone she meets."

"Except her great-nephew," Miss Campbell said,

then bit her lip, looking anxious—as though she had said something she shouldn't.

"Nobody likes William," Edward assured her. "The man's always been an interminable bore and an insufferable know-it-all."

"You know him well?"

"As well as any, I suppose," Edward admitted. "We went to Eton together. I never liked him much. From all I hear of him, he's not much improved."

Miss Campbell laughed softly. "No, I don't think he has."

They stood looking at one another awkwardly for a few moments. Edward supposed that it should be down to him to move the conversation along. But he found himself unusually tongue-tied. He simply did not know what to say. He pursed his lips, then pressed them together, tapped his toe, and wrung his hands nervously. She stood before him, swaying a little from time to time, her eyes looking all around the chamber—anywhere but at him. "I should probably return to the ballroom," he said eventually.

"I suppose you should," she said softly, almost regretfully.

Edward wondered when she had last had someone of her own age to talk with. There were few members of his aunt's household that were of a similar age. Most would either be much younger or much older. She must have found it quite disconcerting to wake up in a strange place, without friends or family—and here she was, at Christmas, just watching everyone else have fun. "Would you like me to stay for a little while longer?" he asked her.

"No, I couldn't ask that of you," she insisted, but her eyes were pleading with him to stay. "I'm not even part of the staff—much less..." she trailed off as if she didn't know how to describe the difference in their social status. Edward wished such things did not matter so much. It made things so very difficult at times, when people felt there were things they could or could not say because of perceived differences between the classes.

"Come, let's sit down before you fall down," he said with a teasing grin. "I can spare half an hour to talk. To tell you the truth, I'm glad to be away from the crowds."

"If you are sure," Miss Campbell said, looking at him with grateful eyes. "I should like that very much."

They walked towards the grand fireplace, where a silk-upholstered sofa and a high-backed leather chair sat opposite one another. Edward took the leather chair and waited for Miss Campbell to settle herself opposite him. She seemed troubled by something, though he didn't know what it might be. "Is there something I can help you with, Miss Campbell?" he asked gently, not wanting to push her too hard on something that she may not want to discuss with a stranger.

"I don't know," she said a little sadly. "I suppose it is quite possible that you might be able to, but I would not wish to trouble you."

"Trouble me," Edward said with an encouraging look.

"I suppose you know your godmother as well as anyone, so you may be able to advise me," Miss Campbell mused.

"Lady Frances?" Edward clarified. Miss Campbell nodded. "She has said something to you?" He couldn't think of anything that his godmother would have been likely to say to this young woman that could possibly be troubling her so. Lady Frances was sweet and generous. He thought it unlikely that she would have given Miss Campbell any ultimatum on how long she might stay— nor was she the kind of woman set any curbs upon any behavior whilst Miss Campbell was under Lady Frances' roof.

"She has asked me to become her companion— permanently," Miss Campbell said, her eyes dipping as though she expected some manner of chastisement for saying such a thing.

"That doesn't surprise me, at all," Edward admitted. "From everything she has told my mother, and what she has said to me, she has grown very fond of you."

"But I simply don't know how to be a lady's companion," Miss Campbell said, her glorious green eyes filling with tears. "I'm not the kind of woman that does such things. I've lived out of a caravan most of my life, moving from place to place as my father cheated and stole his way through life. How could I possibly make a suitable companion for someone like Lady Tremaine?"

Edward chuckled, then stopped himself almost immediately when he saw the genuine concern on Miss Campbell's lovely face. "My dear, I would imagine that your unconventionality is precisely why my godmother would choose you. Have you not noticed that she is a woman that knows her own mind? She lives life her own way. She'd drive a conventional companion to despair—of that I can assure you, as she has done just that when Lord William insisted she take on a companion in the past."

"You truly believe that?"

"I do," Edward said. "She's getting older and can't do as much as she used to. I'm glad she's recognizing that perhaps a companion of her choosing might be just what she needs."

"But I don't even know how to use all the cutlery," Miss Campbell protested. "I don't know how to walk or talk—much less act around toffs like you."

"Not calling us toffs is probably a good place to begin," Edward teased. She flushed and then giggled. "All of those things can be learned. None of us is born knowing them. It takes years of practice—but I have a feeling that you will be a quick study and I know that Lady Frances will be the most patient of teachers."

"You truly think she means it? That she is not just saying such a thing as she feels sorry for me?"

"I doubt that very much. My dear godmother does not suffer fools gladly. She would never suggest you become her companion if she did not truly like you—she'd not set herself up to have to spend time every day with someone who bored her, or she felt needed her charity."

"So, you think I should accept?" Miss Campbell clarified.

"I do, and I will be glad to be of any assistance I can—should you require any additional tutoring," Edward said with a grin.

"Thank you, my Lord," she said. "I cannot tell you how much you have helped to put my mind at ease, and of course, I am grateful for your offer of assistance. I should leave you to return to the party now. It looks wonderful down there."

"You should join us," Edward said encouragingly as she stood up and smoothed down her skirts.

"No, I'm not yet ready to move amongst your kind," she admitted. "Perhaps next year, I may be fit for such company."

She bobbed him another curtsey, then turned and made her way along the gallery, turning to the right when she reached the far end, the entrance to the minstrel's gallery. Edward watched every step she took, mesmerized by the way her hips swayed so rhythmically as she walked, even with her limp. She already walked like a duchess, though she didn't realize it, he thought, her head held high, her frame erect. She also spoke remarkably well, with no clipped vowels or dropped consonants. She had the rich West Country burr, but that could be easily softened. Edward doubted anyone would know the difference between her and someone born and bred to the life of an aristocrat within three months. He looked forward to the challenge and hoped that Lady Frances would not mind his being a frequent visitor to Trelawney Hall to make good on his promise.

Reluctantly, he made his way back down to the ballroom, where he danced with a number of pretty young ladies, fetched them punch, and generally flattered their vanity. But his eyes kept straining upwards, towards the minstrel's gallery, wondering if Miss Campbell was still up there, watching the ball beneath her. He wished he could have convinced her to come down, to dance with him. He would very much like the privilege of holding her in his arms and teaching her the steps—but he had the strongest feeling that she was as proud as a peacock and just as stubborn. She'd not venture into Society until she knew she could pass herself off as a young lady. He vowed to make sure that would happen sooner rather than later.

CHAPTER SIX

New Year had passed. Lady Tremaine had gone to visit with friends of hers in the next county and returned full of plans for a lavish banquet for some of her closest friends to take place on Twelfth Night. Ever since the Christmas Eve ball, Lady Tremaine had begun Anna's lessons in how to be a perfect young lady, and Anna was hopeful that with a little more practice, she would soon be confident enough to attend some of the many events Lady Tremaine had told her of that she would be expected to attend as her companion. She had not, however, expected that day to come quite so quickly.

"I shall present you to my friends tomorrow night," Lady Tremaine said excitedly as she completed another lesson in which set of cutlery accompanied each course in the dining room the day before the supper.

Anna had looked at her aghast. "I am not ready. I don't even know which one is the fish fork," she said, looking back at the array of silverware that had been laid out before her.

"Nonsense. Just work your way inwards or watch whoever you are sat next to for guidance," Lady Tremaine said. "Your table manners are just as good as anyone's, Anna dear. And the sooner you try, the sooner you will get used to being in such company. The people I have invited are sweet and kind. They will not judge you, I promise."

And so, Anna had found herself being introduced to some of the county's finest, wearing a borrowed gown, seated between an earl and a captain of dragoons, and Lady Tremaine had turned out to be quite right—they had been sweet and polite, at least to her face. Nobody had made her feel silly because she didn't know how many tines were on each fork, but she had noticed a number of conversations suddenly halt as she or Lady Tremaine drew near.

Thankfully, as Mrs. Trimble had predicted, Viscount Comey had not even stayed as long as the New Year, and so the evening had been most jolly. However, Anna had been disappointed that the evening had not meant another visit from the handsome Lord Westerham, especially as both his mother and father had been in attendance. The entire event had made her dreadfully nervous, and she had tried to convince herself that she had only been saddened that Lord Westerham had not been present because he would have at least been one face in the crowd that she knew. The evening had been a modest success, and Anna's confidence that she might just be able to make Lady Tremaine an adequate companion had been improved greatly.

They had barely said goodbye to the last of Lady

Tremaine's supper guests on Twelfth Night when she ordered the household to begin packing everything ready for their annual journey to London for the Season. Now, the entire household was in a rush. Maids and manservants rushed hither and thither, their arms filled with all manner of items that would be needed in London. Even as Anna watched the obviously practiced and well-ordered chaos the packing entailed, she had to admit that she had been surprised to learn that someone as unconventional as her new employer would do anything as expected as attend London for the Season, but Anna couldn't help being excited by it.

"Now, we shall have to go to the dressmakers as soon as we arrive," Lady Tremaine said after breakfast, giving Anna's plain gown a derisory glance as she had entered the drawing-room that morning after breakfast. "You will need at least three dresses for morning wear, a riding habit, and..." she paused, tapping her beringed fingers against her lips, "... at least three gowns for evening wear." She walked around Anna, tutting quietly. "And I think it might be an idea to get you a gown for your presentation at court, something with seed pearls, in white."

"Your Ladyship, I am not just a commoner—I'm the daughter of a card sharp. I can't be presented at court," Anna protested. She might have the confidence to perhaps attend a card party, or even a ball before the Season was out, but the idea of being presented at court was a step too far.

"D'you truly think the nobility doesn't have its fair share of cheats and thieves, my dear?" Lady Tremaine asked, raising a single, questioning eyebrow. "Some of them will make your dear departed Da look like a positive angel." Lady Tremaine jabbed Anna in the back, making her stand up straighter. "My dear, all one needs to be presented at court is someone to sponsor you. You do not need wealth or a title. But, if you wish to get anywhere in this world, being presented at court is essential. If Prinny makes you one of his favorites, then quite frankly, Anna, anything might happen. You could even think of making an excellent marriage. Patronage is the real currency in our world—not what you have or who you are—but who you know and who is on your side."

"But I am not looking to make a marriage," Anna protested. "I have barely begun to learn how to be your companion."

Lady Tremaine laughed. "You are a quick study, my dear. You'll not need much longer to have that role perfected. It is always wise for a young woman to think about the future, to be prepared for whatever might come her way."

"You think you might tire of me?" Anna had come to be very fond of her benefactress, and she had no desire to leave her. It stung a little that Lady Tremaine had talked of a time when Anna might wish to leave her, or that Lady Tremaine might no longer want her around.

"Dear Anna," Lady Tremaine said, taking Anna's hand in hers. "I am an old lady. I shall not live forever. You cannot assume that William will continue to find a role for you within the household once he inherits all. I would much rather know that you are safe and well—and if possible, happy—long before I pass off this mortal coil."

Anna shook her head as if she could somehow ward

off Lady Tremaine's passing with her denial. But the more she thought about it, the more she realized that the older woman was quite right. Anna had been left alone when her father had passed. There would come a day when Lady Tremaine would not be there to protect her, to employ her, or to care for her. Anna had to be wise and think ahead. She could not bear to face the emptiness she had felt as she'd trudged along the road to Winchester, with nothing and nobody to care for. Nor did she ever wish to find herself penniless and without hope ever again.

"Now, be a good girl," Lady Tremaine said with a gentle smile and a gentle squeeze of Anna's arm, signaling that their talk was now over. "Go and fetch my wrap from my bedchamber. There is a bit of a chill in the air. The last thing I need is to be unwell when we arrive in London."

Anna fetched the wrap then returned to Lady Tremaine's chambers where she spent the rest of the afternoon assisting the maids to fold and press every garment Lady Tremaine wished to take to London, to wrap them in velvet then pack them into the awaiting trunks. She'd never realized that one woman could own so many garments. By the time every undergarment, every gown, every shoe, and every coat was packed, there were four large trunks filled, and a fifth, only slightly smaller one, contained all of Lady Tremaine's perfumes, powders, creams, hairbrushes, pins, and jewelry.

Anna was utterly fagged by the time she got to her bed that night. The doctor had said he was happy that her leg had set well and was healing much more quickly than he would have expected. But he had insisted that it remain in the splints during the daytime for another couple of weeks to be certain. Anna still got some pain and limped a little, though she had stopped using the cane. She unbandaged the leg and massaged it absent-mindedly as she wondered what it would be like to be in London.

She'd never been there before. Pa had never ventured so far from the world he knew, here in the west of England. Anna imagined fancy carriages, women in fine dresses, men dressed in top hats and tailcoats, all nodding to one another politely. She wondered what Lady Tremaine's new house on Berkeley Square would be like; would it be large, but comfortable, filled with the accumulation of family treasures handed down from generation to generation like Trelawney Hall, or would it be the very height of modern fashion? She lay back against the pillows, closed her eyes, and drifted off to sleep, dreaming of the adventures and excitement that was to follow.

In the morning, when Anna awoke, it was raining heavily. She sighed heavily, stretched and, after re-bandaging her bad leg, she got up and dressed swiftly, before hurrying downstairs to see if there was anything more that needed to be done before they set out for London. Cook was busy packing up the last of her things, the ones she'd needed to make supper last night and breakfast this morning. She beamed at Anna. "I'm told the new kitchen will have everything a cook could ever dream of having," she said. "Can you imagine? I'll hardly know what I'm about."

"I am sure we will all learn how to deal with the newfangled world," Anna said with a wry smile as she thought about all the new things she was learning, the people she would have to meet, and the places she would be visiting very soon.

"Indeed, you have more than most to be getting used to," Cook said thoughtfully. "You'll do well, though. Don't you doubt it."

"I'm more suited to being below stairs, with you and everyone else."

"You've a chance to make something of yourself, Anna love. Don't you let that pass you by because you feel a bit out of place. There are hundreds, nay thousands, of girls who would love to have the opportunities you have ahead of you. Don't you be afraid of 'em. You've faced harder and survived it."

"If it all goes dreadfully wrong, may I come and work for you here in the kitchens?" Anna said, only half-joking. "If I embarrass myself in some terrible way."

"Aye, you'll be right," Cook said reassuringly. "But Lady Tremaine'll never let you be left out in the cold. She'll do right by you, whatever happens. Now, go on with you. I'll wager there'll be a lesson this morning in how to eat a boiled egg with a dainty silver spoon awaiting you."

"Because you prepared boiled eggs for breakfast, perchance?" Anna said with a grin. Cook grinned and then nodded her head in a way that told Anna she was done with her.

Upstairs, people were still rushing back and forth, carrying all manner of items, from lamps and blankets to mangles and coal scuttles. Anna entered the breakfast room and found Lady Tremaine sitting at the table, reading a letter. "Good morning," Anna said as she entered.

Lady Tremaine looked up from her correspondence. "Good morning to you," she said. "Now, I want you to pour the chocolate this morning, the way I showed you yesterday."

Anna felt the familiar buzz of nerves in the pit of her stomach that she felt every time Lady Tremaine asked her to show how well she had learned a new skill. She moved to the sideboard where a tray sat with three different silver pots arranged upon it, with three different sets of cups and saucers. The pot to the left was tall and had a short spout and a long handle. The one in the center was squatter, and more rounded, and the final pot was tall like the first pot, but with a much longer spout and shorter handle.

Pausing for a moment, Anna thought about which one she needed, trying to remember everything that Lady Tremaine had taught her. It didn't take her long to decide upon the pot to the left of the tray. Then she looked at the different cups set out before her. The set that was in front of the chocolate pot was short, with a wide brim and a narrow base; she was sure that they would be most suitable for tea. Those in front of the shorter pot were taller and more cylindrical so she was sure they were intended for coffee.

Which meant that the cups in front of the tall pot on the right-hand side of the tray, with their tall and narrow shape, and their lids and two handles, were the ones she required. She arranged the cups onto their matching saucers then pulled the silver chocolate pot towards her. "Are you sure that is the chocolate pot?" Lady Tremaine asked nonchalantly.

"I am," Anna said. "The spout is shorter and the handle longer than that of the coffee pot—and the teapot is much shorter and fatter than the coffee pot, so this must be the chocolate pot. I can also smell the vanilla and the spices, so I am sure this is the correct pot."

"And why have you chosen those particular cups and saucers?"

"Because chocolate is served in a..." Anna paused as she tried to remember the fancy name for them. "...a *trembleuse*," she said, proud of herself for remembering.

"Well done," Lady Tremaine said as Anna brought the now filled cups to the table. Anna smiled at her praise. She tried so very hard to get things right, and it was so hard to do so when there was so much to learn.

Anna took her seat, trying to remember the way Lady Tremaine had showed her, and smiled as one of the maids brought her a plate of, as Cook had predicted, boiled eggs set in pretty china egg cups. Lady Tremaine took up a special knife and expertly sliced off the top of her egg, laying it to the side, and then picked up a tiny silver spoon, which she dipped into the egg, then shook off the drips of yolk before raising it to her lips.

Anna thought that it all looked simple enough. She picked up the knife and tried to slice the top off her egg, as Lady Tremaine had done. The egg cracked a little but certainly did not slice off in the neat and precise manner that Lady Tremaine's had done. Anna took a deep breath and tried again. This time she was able to pierce through the eggshell, but the top of the egg came away in a ragged way, leaving sharp shards of shell poking up that she had to carefully remove with her fingers before dipping in her spoon. "I shall never learn everything in time," Anna moaned.

"Of course you will," Lady Tremaine said encouragingly. "You did that far better than I did the first time I ever tried. It took me almost three years to master this particular skill. It comes with practice—and as you will only be eating breakfast with me for some time to come, I do not think it is a skill you need worry yourself over."

Anna nodded. Sometimes it all seemed overwhelming; every single thing she had ever known she had to unlearn, and then learn something completely new—and often, to her mind, utterly silly. Just over a month ago, she had been a penniless girl in desperate need of a position. Within moments, her life had changed. Being knocked over by that dreadful phaeton, breaking her leg, and finding herself here at Trelawney Hall had been change enough. That she was now learning how to be a young lady in Society seemed almost unreal.

It all seemed somehow too good to be true, that a girl like her could be seated at a table like this, surrounded by silver and china and fine fabrics and good food. She'd been hungry and cold most of her life. Now she slept in a warm and comfortable bed every night, in a dry and warm room of her own. She was to be bought a number of gowns and was expected to wear them to all manner of events and functions once they were in London. Anna felt the pressure to be ready, to do everything as she should—because she never wanted Lady Tremaine to feel she had made the wrong decision. Anna owed the kindly older woman her life, and she would give all she had to repay that debt. If that meant she had to master removing the top of an egg seamlessly, then it was a small price to pay.

"The carriage will be ready at ten o'clock. I want to leave promptly," Lady Tremaine said, returning to her letter. "We have a long journey ahead of us. I have arranged for us to stay at a coaching inn overnight, but we should be in London before dark tomorrow evening."

"I shall ensure that everyone is ready," Anna assured her.

CHAPTER SEVEN

"You will be there this evening, won't you, Westerham?" Lord Carlton Sable asked Edward as he rose up out of his chair and started to put on the hat and coat that the liveried servant who stood before him was holding out to him. The Carlton Club was quiet this afternoon, but that had been to the two friends' benefit as they caught up on one another's news. Sable was one of Edward's oldest friends. They had gone to Eton together and on their Grand Tour—and he was always the first person Edward sought out once he arrived in the capital city.

Sable had pulled on his coat and was toying with his top hat. "I don't think I can face my mother alone. She is always so disappointed in me. She loves you, Westerham, so if you are there, she may forget to be so let down by my failings."

Edward laughed. Sable had always been one to exaggerate how much his mother despised him, but dining with them was often a pleasant enough affair. "I should be delighted to join your family for supper. Please tell your mother that I am most grateful for the invitation."

Sable put on his top hat, took his cane from the servant and gave Edward a friendly wink. "You are a top fellow," he said, tapping the end of the cane twice upon the table. "I shall see you at half-past seven, and do not be late. You know that Father can be a dreadful ogre about tardiness." He turned and marched out of the club, leaving Edward still sitting in his chair, grinning.

"Can I fetch you anything, my Lord?" the servant asked, giving Edward a perfunctory bow.

"My hat and coat, Holdsworth. Thank you," Edward said. The man disappeared, and Edward picked up his brandy glass and drank the last mouthful of the rich, golden liquid. He set the glass back down and pulled out the note he had received that morning at breakfast. He read his godmother's words with pleasure. She and Miss Campbell were finally settled into the Berkeley Square house and would be delighted to receive him for tea this very afternoon. He glanced at his pocket watch. It was still only two o'clock. Lady Frances' invitation stipulated he should attend them at three. He still had time to get across town, and then back again to join his friend for supper.

Holdsworth brought his things, and Edward left the club. London was busy, as always. He walked briskly along the street twirling his cane in a nonchalant manner. He felt happy to be back. He always thought that this was where he most belonged, amongst all the hustle and bustle. He didn't much like having to attend all the dreary events his mother insisted he make an appearance at, but he did like spending time at his club and attending the opera and the ballet. However, none of those things were responsible for his good mood. No, he thought as he hailed a hansom cab, that was entirely because of his destination and the people he would see once he arrived there.

He'd been surprised at how often Miss Campbell had crossed his thoughts since they had met on Christmas Eve. He wondered how her lessons in deportment, elocution, and manners were coming along. He had no doubt that Lady Frances would make an excellent and most patient tutor—but he had the strongest feeling that Miss Campbell might not be such a temperate pupil. Something about her told Edward that she could be quite fiery, and he was sure that she had a strong desire to please. If she felt she was letting anyone down, Edward felt sure that would be quite upsetting for her.

Reaching the tall and imposing house on one of the most newly fashionable squares in London, Edward bounded up the steps, took the brass door knocker in his hand, and knocked loudly on the door with three smart raps. He stood back, leaning against the cast-iron railings, and looked around the square. It really was very smart. The Palladian architecture set off the perfectly manicured green park in the center. It was a quiet and leafy place, given that they were so close to the hubbub of the City of London itself.

The door opened. Harker, Lady Frances' butler, appeared, his lined face familiar and welcoming to Edward. "Come in, my Lord," he said with a bow. "Her

Ladyship is awaiting you in the drawing-room. If you'll follow me?"

Edward looked up and around him as they crossed the marble-floored hallway. A grand oak staircase arose through the center of the space, its elegantly carved woodwork a testament to its creator's craftsmanship. A couple of large portraits hung on the walls, set beside a number of landscapes and seascapes. A large bust sat on a plinth by a vast armoire, and a handsome grandfather clock chimed the hour as they reached the door of the drawing-room. Harker opened the door and ushered him inside.

Lady Frances was sat beside the fireplace on a sofa upholstered in a striped green damask. Miss Campbell sat beside her. They were poring over a book together and were so engrossed in their task that they did not seem to have even noticed that he had entered the room. He cleared his throat loudly. "Ahem."

"Edward, do be a dear and call for some tea," Lady Frances said, still not looking up.

"I say, standards of hospitality have dropped since last I came if a chap has to order his own tea," he teased.

Miss Campbell looked up. She looked chagrined. "I can do it," she said, moving to stand up.

"Not at all. Edward is being facetious," Lady Frances said briskly. "You have more important things to do than to order tea. Edward has all the time in the world and nothing to fill it. Let him be useful for once."

"You wound me," Edward said, dramatically clasping his hands to his chest and feigning the pain of injury. Miss Campbell laughed.

"Do be a good boy, for once, Edward. Miss Campbell and I are at a crucial point in her lesson. I didn't for one instant think you would come on time, you never have before, so do forgive me if we aren't quite ready for you," Lady Frances said with a withering glance.

Edward chuckled and went back out into the hallway, where he called out for a maid. One came scuttling out of the dining room, bobbing a curtsey as she hurried to his side. "How may I help you, my Lord?" she asked breathlessly.

"Tea for three, in the drawing-room, and if Cook has some of her wonderful seed cake, I would be most delighted to see some upon the tray," Edward said, giving her a cheeky wink. The maid blushed from her neck to her temples and giggled a little before she turned and ran away down a dark corridor Edward could only assume led to the stairs down to the kitchens.

As his godmother and Miss Campbell were still otherwise engaged, Edward decided to explore the new house. He knew Lady Frances had spent a small fortune on it, and he was curious to see what that money had been spent on. He wandered from room to room downstairs, marveling at the light and bright rooms with their high ceilings and decorative plasterwork. He made his way upstairs and peeked inside the rooms there, bedchambers, studies, dressing rooms—each one perfectly appointed. Each one with a distinct and personal character.

When he heard a bell ring downstairs, he hurried back down and re-entered the drawing-room. Whilst Lady Frances was still sitting where he'd left her, Miss

Campbell was on her feet, carefully arranging the tea things on the table. Edward moved forward to greet his godmother properly. She stood up and embraced him warmly. "Dear Edward, thank you for coming to visit with us," she said, as he kissed her on the cheek.

"You invited me, and so I came," he said affectionately. "I am yours to command, as you well know."

"I am glad to hear it," Lady Frances said as she sat back down and indicated he should sit beside her. He obliged her and leaned back against the comfortable sofa, stretching his legs out in front of him. "For we have need of you."

"You do?" Edward asked, looking from his godmother to Miss Campbell, feeling that he was not party to some important piece of information that he really should know.

"Don't look so frightened. It isn't anything dreadful, or too onerous for a feckless soul like you." Lady Frances smiled at Miss Campbell as she walked forwards and handed her a cup of tea. Edward couldn't help noticing how much smoother her gait was now, and how beautifully she held herself. Obviously, much had changed since they had met at Christmas.

"I am glad to hear it," he admitted, not taking his eyes off Miss Campbell as she walked back to the table to fetch him a cup of tea, too. "I should so hate to lose my reputation for fecklessness."

"Would you care for some cake?" Miss Campbell asked him as she passed him his cup and saucer. "It isn't the seed cake you requested, but plum cake. It is very good. Cook uses lots of cinnamon."

"It sounds delightful," Edward said.

Miss Campbell carefully took the knife and sliced the cake into equal tranches, sliding one onto a plate with deft hands, which she then brought over to him. "Doesn't she do that well?" Lady Frances said, sounding delighted.

"She does," he admitted, then noticed that Miss Campbell was not limping and nor was she unsteady on her feet. "You are looking very well, Miss Campbell. I can see that you are healing very well now. I presume serving tea is just one of the skills the pair of you have been working on?"

"Thank you, it is," Miss Campbell said, bringing her cup over and sitting on a chair opposite his godmother. She perched on the edge of the seat with her knees pressed together and her back as straight as a poker, as if she had never slouched a day in her life.

"I have been teaching Anna to read and to write, and all of the skills that a young lady needs in Society," Lady Frances said with a smile. "And she is a very quick study. But there is one skill that we need a little assistance with, and that is dancing. So, would you mind coming each morning so that we may teach her the most common dances?"

Edward chuckled. He'd not been expecting that. "I would be delighted," he said, and meant it. From the first night he'd met her, it had been his desire to do just that. "Though I cannot come every day. I have matters I must attend to. Would Tuesdays and Thursdays be sufficient?"

"You don't mind?" Miss Campbell asked, her beautiful green eyes filled with anxiety.

"Not at all, and once my dear godmother deems you

fit for a public dance, I can assure you that I will be the first man there to mark your card."

Miss Campbell smiled shyly. "You are both too kind," she said. "I do not deserve such attention."

"Of course you do," Lady Frances said briskly. "It is hardly your fault if you were born a pauper. Any one of us could have been cursed with such a start in life. It is what you do with your life once you are born that matters, and I see a much more promising future for you than that which you were born to. Now, I am tired after our lessons this morning, so I shall leave you both now whilst I take a short nap. When I come back down, I shall expect Anna to know the steps to at least one reel, Edward." She gave him a stern look, then unable to hold the serious expression, she grinned. "I shall send Harker in to play for you; he can play the violin passably well."

Edward smiled and watched her leave. She truly was the most unpredictable of characters. "She is quite a woman," he said softly.

"She certainly is. I do not know why she has taken me under her wing in the way she has, but I will be eternally grateful for it," Miss Campbell said.

She sipped at her tea, and Edward popped a forkful of cake into his mouth to hide the fact that he didn't know what to say next. The silence was almost palpable between them, until Harker entered the room carrying a violin in one hand and the bow in his other. "Her Ladyship said you required me to play?" he said, raising his eyebrows quizzically.

"Indeed," Edward said. "She wishes Miss Campbell to learn to dance, so something lively I think to start." He stood up and started to move the furniture back against the wall. "You could help me clear a suitable space, too," he added, looking meaningfully at the butler, who was still stood in the doorway.

Harker set down his instrument and rushed forward. Miss Campbell cleared away the tea things and began to help them to move the rugs and the couches. "No, you are to learn to be a young lady," Edward cautioned her. "No young lady would ever move furniture."

"But there is nobody here that would know. I cannot just stand here and do nothing," she complained. "I may be learning to be a young lady, but I was not born one. I am happy to work for my keep, and you, my Lord, should not be doing such manual labor, either."

"I suppose you have got me there," Edward admitted. "I will not tell if you do not?" he said, giving her a meaningful glance before looking at Harker. "And I expect you to keep this to yourself, too."

"My lord, I do not know what you might be referring to," Harker said, obviously trying hard to keep a straight face. "I moved the furniture alone."

They all grinned, and in no time had cleared a space suitable for dancing. Harker took up his violin and began to play a lively tune. Edward showed Miss Campbell the steps first, at the tempo that would be expected of her at a dance. She watched closely, her cat-like eyes not missing a single thing. He loved her intensity; it was utterly refreshing. When Edward thought about the young women he had known in his life, intensity was not a word that could ever have been used to describe them. Vain, perhaps, skittish, most certainly—and quite often distracted, too.

He offered Miss Campbell his hand in a gallant gesture, inviting her onto the makeshift dancefloor. She held out her hand prettily and placed it in his. Edward was surprised to feel a surge of sensation flood through him at such an innocent touch. He looked down into her lovely face. She looked up at him, her eyes wide. Neither looked away, the connection between them was too magnetic, until Harker played the opening chord of the song, and they broke away, their hands falling to their sides as they tried to make sense of what it was that had just passed between them. Miss Campbell looked away, turning her whole head from him and Edward shook his head to try to clear his suddenly jumbled thoughts.

"After the first chord, the lady curtseys," he managed to say. Miss Campbell dipped into as graceful a curtsey as Edward had ever seen. "And then the man bows." He bent at the waist and then stood up straight. He offered her his hand again. She hesitated, but finally placed her hand upon his, and he began to teach her the steps and got her to go through them slowly, repeating each one over and over again. His aunt was right; she was a quick study. In no time at all, she seemed to have learned the entire dance and was performing it with natural grace.

"You must have danced before," he marveled as she insisted they learn another.

"Not like this," she said. "But I watched everyone at the ball at Christmas, and I must confess, I tried to dance along with the caller. I so wanted to be a part of it;

everyone looked so happy. All those fine gowns and men in their colorful jackets. I'd never seen anything like it."

"You've never been to a dance?" Edward asked. "You just learned everything by watching?"

"When you can't read or write or afford teachers, it's the only way to learn anything," Miss Campbell said with a rueful smile. "And I've been to dances, or rather I've danced at weddings and fayres and such like. But we don't dance the way your kind do. It's all a little more raucous—much less refined."

"I should like to see that someday," Edward said.

"I doubt you'd ever find yourself in the kind of places where such things would take place," Miss Campbell said just as Lady Frances returned from her nap.

"So, are you going to show me?" she demanded, taking her seat on one of the couches up against the wall.

"We shall. I think you will be very pleased with Miss Campbell's progress," Edward said and nodded to Harker, who struck up the chord for them to begin. Yet, even as they danced together, something had changed. Miss Campbell could no longer bring herself to look at him. It was obvious, even though she danced the steps perfectly, that the mood of exploration had been replaced with a more perfunctory one, focused entirely upon displaying her new-found skill.

Edward had danced with many young women. Dancing with Miss Campbell before his godmother's reappearance had been nothing like the experiences he'd had before. He knew that he was not wrong; there had been a genuine connection between them. Yet now, it was as if he were dancing with anyone. The light seemed to have gone out in Miss Campbell's eyes. She was trying so hard to be what Lady Frances wanted of her. As they broke apart to his godmother's applause, Edward found himself praying that all the lessons wouldn't completely strip Miss Campbell of who she truly was inside.

E aster came and went, and Edward reluctantly
attended Court at the request of his dear friend,
Prinny. He'd been surprised to find himself being
ushered upstairs to a gallery above the throne room, and
that there seemed to be chattering huddle of young
women waiting for the arrival of Queen Charlotte and
her son. It had soon dawned upon him that this must be
one of the days where the royal family greeted the young
women who wished to come out into Society, and he
sighed. He'd not be seeing Prinny to find out why he was
here for some time.

The Prince Regent seemed to fluctuate between
enjoying the formality of such traditions and despising
the silliness of it all, and Edward could easily understand
why. From his raised vantage point above the grand presence chamber, Edward was able to watch as the vast
crowd of women in white were herded towards the dais
where Prinny and Queen Charlotte sat on gilded
thrones. He watched as mothers fussed around their over-

dressed offspring, adjusting elaborate hairstyles and fidgeting with gleaming jewels and great fat pearls to be sure that their charges were utterly perfect for their moment with the royal family and was heartily glad that he had been born a man.

Queen Charlotte still insisted that the girls wear gowns with hooped skirts, even though modern fashions most certainly did not suit such undergarments, and the chamber beneath appeared cramped, though the guest list was quite small, as the elaborate gowns took up so much more space than their inhabitants. Edward had heard tales of gowns for the event costing five hundred pounds or more. He was beginning to understand why, as he considered the reams of material and the hours of work undertaken by seamstresses required to sew on the thousands of beads and seed pearls that accentuated the embroidery at bodice and hem. Such extravagance was not afforded by many, especially when such gowns would only ever be worn once, for this very occasion.

The line of young women snaked its way across the chamber towards the dais, each young woman getting their few moments to be greeted by Prinny and the Queen. Edward wanted to laugh as he saw their solemn faces and how seriously they were all taking the moment. He was surprised that Prinny was able to keep such a straight face himself, but he remained somber, undertaking his duties with gravitas Edward had rarely seen in his fast-living friend. Edward was not sure why Prinny had summoned him here tonight, and he wished the endless pageantry below were over so he might find out.

Edward had never seen the presentation of young

women at Court before. The vacuity of it all seemed a little pointless to him, yet it was a tradition that seemed to endure. Young women could only attend if they were introduced by a woman already presented at Court themselves. Often, girls were presented by their mothers or aunts. But occasionally, some young women were introduced by others amongst their social circles. It was said that being presented at Court could improve one's chances of marriage, but Edward didn't understand why and nor did he much care.

Tapping his feet impatiently as he prayed for the spectacle below to be over, Edward tried to think why so many people longed to attend one of these very select events. He'd known Prinny most of his life. Edward's father had been one of King George's closest advisors until he had been struck down with his mysterious illness. The boys had spent a lot of time together, and though Prinny was a few years older than Edward was, he had always been supportive and kind to the younger boy. Their friendship, and that of their fathers, had made life very easy for Edward. He supposed that these young women hoped for a little bit of favor of their own, though Edward couldn't help thinking that there must be better ways to achieve it.

It was strange, Edward thought as he continued to watch girl after girl drop into a deep curtsey and waited to be raised by the queen, that he had not recognized a single one of the girls here this afternoon. This was the very last of these afternoon events for the Season, though, so Edward supposed that these were perhaps the daughters of those not so in favor with Prinny and Queen Charlotte so had been unable to be presented at the earlier events in the Season. Given his place in Society, it was not entirely surprising that he wouldn't know these daughters of merchants and other lowlier, but often wealthier, members of Society. These people inhabited a tier of the very hierarchical world that he did not have much to do with.

Finally, when the ceremony was almost over, there was a face he knew all too well approaching the dais. His godmother, Lady Frances, introduced Miss Campbell to Prinny and the queen. Lady Frances was clad in a gown that seemed to extend outwards at least as wide as she was tall. She had a tall wig, with flowers and peacock feathers poking out of it, and her face was powdered. Edward had never seen his godmother conform to anything before, and it made him smile.

Miss Campbell stood next to her. She looked dreadfully nervous and was biting on her lip in the way she always did when she wasn't entirely sure she was where she thought she should be. Her loveliness made Edward's heart stop. Miss Campbell had somehow managed to make the obligatory ostentatious gown she wore look lovely. Her hair had been pinned prettily, but she had eschewed the elaborate dressing that every other woman present had adopted, and she wore no rouge from what Edward could see. Her gown was not much wider than her hips, though it was clear she was wearing the appropriate hoop beneath, and it had only minimal adornments. She looked natural and lovely, and Edward was glad to see what must have been a very proud moment for her and his aunt.

So that was why Prinny had summoned him. Edward had spoken with his friend about his godmother and her companion just the other night, and Prinny had been quick to perceive Edward's fondness for Miss Campbell. He was a sweet man, Edward thought. That he'd remembered such a brief conversation and then made sure that Edward could be a part of what was a very important occasion for the two women he cared most about in the world. And Prinny confirmed his suspicions by looking up to the gallery and giving him a conspiratorial wink. Edward grinned at him and raised his hands to offer his old friend a silent round of applause. Prinny looked delighted with himself, and his work finally done, escorted his mother from the presence chamber.

Edward made his way downstairs into the grand hallway of the palace. Some of the young women and their mothers were still milling around. Others had begun to make their way out into the spring sunshine to wait for their carriages to be brought round. He looked eagerly for any sign of Miss Campbell and his godmother, using his height to good advantage to peer over the heads of the many women surrounding him. He located them, stood by a bust of King George, talking with another young woman that seemed a little bit familiar, though Edward did not know why.

He approached them cautiously. He did not wish to disturb them if they were deep in conversation, but Lady Frances spotted him before he'd even gotten halfway across the hall. He grinned at her. She looked delighted to see him and waited impatiently as he took the final few steps to be by their side. He bowed politely to her, Miss

Campbell, and to the young woman who was with them. But such a perfunctory greeting was not sufficient for the exuberantly happy Lady Frances. "Edward, what a lovely surprise," she cried, reaching up so she might take his face in her hands, then pressing kisses to both of his cheeks. He felt his cheeks flush but didn't complain. In fact, he put his arms around her and gave her a fond hug.

"Prinny summoned me," he said truthfully. "I should go and find him to see why, but I couldn't let you go without coming to pay my respects."

"Have you met Miss Mary Cordwainer, my Lord?" Miss Campbell said, introducing the young woman stood beside her.

Edward wracked his brains, then it came to him. He vaguely recalled that he'd seen her name in the newspaper announcing an engagement to Captain Elliot Winters. "I don't believe we have met, but I believe congratulations are in order, Miss Cordwainer? I hear you have become affianced to Captain Elliot Winters?"

Miss Cordwainer blushed prettily. "We are to be wed before the end of the Season."

"He is a very lucky man, indeed."

"I think so," Miss Campbell said, tucking an arm through the young woman's arm. "Mary has been the very best of friends to me since we came to London."

"If you will excuse me," Lady Frances said unexpectedly. "Mary, I must take you and introduce you to an old friend of mine before your carriage arrives and your mother whisks you away. Do you mind if I leave you to watch over Anna for me, Edward? She has been so nervous about being here."

"Not at all," Edward assured his godmother. "I shall guard her with my life. Perhaps I could even show her a little of the palace. I'm sure Prinny won't mind." He was rewarded with a delighted smile from Miss Campbell at the suggestion, and he thought his coming here and suffering through that interminably long ceremony was suddenly all worth it.

"You call him Prinny?" Miss Cordwainer said, her mouth dropping open with her surprise at such informality.

"Indeed, I've known him since I was a boy," Edward explained. "I know this palace almost as well as I do my own home."

Mary was still open-mouthed as Lady Frances steered her away, and Edward offered Miss Campbell his arm. "So, you managed to fool royalty, too," he teased.

"Who else have I fooled?" she asked, looking a little put-out.

"At least half, if not all, of the *ton*," Edward said and laughed softly. "There isn't a soul I know that even suspects that you might not be what you seem."

"And what is it that I seem, my Lord?" Miss Campbell asked him, her eyes narrowing, her tone waspish.

"A young lady of good breeding and fine manners, born to the Society in which you have been so delightfully flitting through for the past weeks."

"We both know I am nothing of the sort."

"But nobody else does—and perception is all in this world, dear Miss Campbell. I cannot tell you how impressed I am at your achievements."

Miss Campbell sighed heavily. "To tell you the truth,

Lord Westerham, I am weary of all of it. I know that Lady Tremaine is quite giddy at her success in turning me into something I am not, but I long to wear a gown that doesn't need me to be laced into a corset, to be able to slouch when I sit down—and to be able to pick up a chicken leg with my fingers and gnaw on it like a dog. I have to eat such small portions of everything that I am forever half-starved."

Edward steered her towards a corridor at the rear of the hallway. "The secret is to eat as much as you can before you go anywhere," he told her solemnly. "Then you won't be so hungry, or so tired."

"I shall remember that, though I do not think we will be in London much longer."

"You don't?" Edward asked anxiously. He'd not realized, even though he was well aware of how much he liked and respected Miss Campbell, just how much he would miss her if she were not here. She'd come to be the highlight of his time here in London.

"Lady Tremaine hides it well, but she is tired," Miss Campbell said. "I worry about her health. She refuses to admit that she needs any help, won't let me call the doctor, but underneath the powder she dusts so liberally over her skin, she is pale as a ghost, and she naps longer every day. I am worried about her."

"But if she is refusing assistance, then surely she will not agree to go back to the country?"

"She has been invited by some friends to go to Bath earlier than planned this year. When she sent her acceptance of their invitation, I knew then that she was ailing much more than she was telling me." Miss Campbell's words were innocent enough, but Edward thought he saw a flicker of something more in her eyes. She had proven to him over and over again that she was clever and quick, and full of guile. Edward couldn't help but wonder if the invitation from Lady Frances' friends had, in some way, been pre-empted.

"Their intervention was most fortuitous," Edward said with a grin.

"Indeed," she said, then realizing he knew what she'd done, she grinned back. "I worry about her. She has been so very good to me. I hope you do not mind that I wanted to take care of her."

"Why ever would I mind your wanting to do that?" Edward asked as he opened the door of a quiet and cozy parlor. Books lined one of the walls, and large windows looked out over the perfectly manicured knot garden and on to the park beyond.

"Viscount Comey was not happy when Lady Tremaine mentioned she might be leaving town," Miss Campbell said and frowned. "It is as if he wants her to be here, to wear herself out, and to make herself sick so he might inherit sooner. The man is the most dreadful bounder."

They both stared out of the window for some time. If anyone had seen them, they would have said they were close enough to touch, but the voluminous skirts of Miss Campbell's court dress meant that the gap felt as wide as the ocean to Edward. He longed to take her hand, to tell her how he truly felt—but he knew he could not. He knew that he should not. It would be wrong of him. His father would never approve of a match between them.

Miss Campbell could bring nothing to a marriage: no dowry, no land. But knowing he could not have her for his own did not make being near her any easier.

Other, less scrupulous, men might have taken advantage of a girl like Miss Campbell. They'd think nothing of promising her the moon and stars, taking her maidenhead, and then leaving her to face the consequences alone should a child result from their indiscretion. Edward would never do that to her, or to anyone. He loved her, and he wanted the very best for her. He couldn't bear to think of her being with anyone but him, but he knew that if the time came—and the man was good enough for her—that he would gladly celebrate her engagement. She deserved a fine life.

A door behind them creaked as it was flung wide. Edward and Miss Campbell both turned to see Prinny hurrying across the parlor towards them. "Ah, dear Miss Campbell—and my old friend. I am so glad both of you were able to attend today. Wasn't it a wonderful day?"

"It was, Your Highness," Miss Campbell said, dropping into a deep curtsey that she did not get up from.

"Do get up," Prinny said, a hint of exasperation in his voice. "I've seen enough of the tops of people's heads for today."

"Yes, Your Highness," Miss Campbell said, rising to her feet as Prinny reached out and shook Edward's hand firmly. He reached out and clapped Edward fondly on the back, then stood back, put his fleshy hands upon his rotund belly, and looked at them both with keen eyes.

"Westerham here tells me that you are a very fine dancer," Prinny said. "Now, I shall have to hope that is indeed true, as I have already made sure that my name is on your dance card for tonight's ball. I do hope I won't tread on your toes too much."

Miss Campbell flushed as red as a beet and fidgeted a little. Edward gave her a reassuring smile. He knew she was anxious about the evening's entertainments. But she rallied well. "I shall be honored," she said bravely.

"I should escort Miss Campbell home now," Edward said to his friend. "She will want to rest and be ready for the ball, especially if she is to be dodging your great feet, Your Highness."

"I'm afraid I can't spare you," Prinny said, sinking into one of the vast sofas by the fireplace. "I have need of your counsel, so though you may escort your delightful friend back to Lady Tremaine and to their carriage, I'd rather like it if you'd come back straight away, my old friend."

Edward bowed and did as he asked. It was hard to part with both women when their carriage pulled up outside. Knowing that this may be one of the last times they would be able to spend time together made it feel poignant and sad. But Prinny never asked him for anything, though he had given Edward so much over the years. Edward could not let his friend down, even if it meant he missed out on precious moments with Lady Frances, and especially with Miss Campbell.

He waved them off and then hurried back to the parlor where he'd left Prinny. When he returned, Prinny was pacing up and down. "I don't know what to do," he said before Edward had even closed the door behind him.

"About what, exactly?"

"It is, a little coincidentally, to do with Lady Tremaine," Prinny said, his eyes cautiously searching Edward's face, his body tense. It was quite clear to Edward that the news his old friend was about to impart was bad and might, in some way, harm Lady Frances. "Though not directly."

Edward felt his insides begin to churn. "Tell me, Prinny. Whatever is wrong?"

"That dratted idiot, Comey," Prinny said, disdain dripping from his voice. The Prince Regent had never liked Comey either, but he wasn't usually so obviously venomous when he spoke of him. In truth, Edward couldn't think of a time when the prince had so much as mentioned him since they were boys. If Comey was up to something, then Prinny was only involving himself because of Lady Tremaine, whom he had a soft spot for. They were both delightfully eccentric, so had always got along well.

Prinny took a deep breath and looked Edward in the eye. "I hear he's gotten himself into some trouble. Rumor has it that there is to be a duel, somewhere. I can't go and stop it—but you can."

CHAPTER NINE

The next week passed swiftly. Lord Westerham called at the house to teach Anna more dances twice a week, and he joined her and Lady Tremaine for lunch after each lesson, where he was polite and circumspect, and Anna could not have faulted him on his manners at any time. Yet it always felt as if there was something he wasn't saying, something he wanted to tell her but couldn't. She certainly knew that there was something she wished she could confess to him. She longed to tell him just how glad she was that he had been there for her presentation at court. Just seeing his smiling face in that crowd had made her feel so very reassured that she belonged there.

She couldn't help reminiscing about their dancing lessons, especially that first one all those weeks ago now. The mood between them, the way he had truly seen her —not just the creature Lady Tremaine wished her to become—and had not turned away. She wanted to tell him how just the touch of his hand had given her shivers, and that she had felt a peculiar prickling all over just being close to him.

But she was a servant. He was a lord and would one day be an earl, and so she must never speak of it. Even though Lady Tremaine had high hopes of her making a good match, such a man as Lord Westerham would never see a woman like her as a possible wife. No, when she'd talked of such things, Lady Tremaine had meant that perhaps Anna might find an officer or a merchant who might wish to marry her—she'd not ever meant her dear godson. It would behoove Anna to remember that each time he took her hand and led her through the steps of a new dance, each time her mind wandered into the realms of fantasy that one day he would choose to dance with only her.

As Anna's skills had grown, she had begun to accompany Lady Tremaine to some of the many engagements she was invited to, and Anna had taken that as a compliment to how far she had come that she was learning things well enough to be seen in public. Anna had made a number of friends whom she went walking with in the mornings, or to tea with in the afternoons. As well as attending her Coming Out, and the ball that evening, she and Lady Tremaine had been to a talk on butterflies given at the museum and to the opera to see something by a gentleman called Mozart. It had been utterly overwhelming. Anna had never experienced such a range of emotions in such a short space of time. The ballet and the theatre had both been just as enlightening and enjoyable, though emotionally exhausting. They had also attended a number of card parties, where Lady Tremaine had warned Anna not to try any of the practices her father had taught her. Anna had assured her that she had never had much of a gift for sleight of hand and that she would never dream of doing anything that might embarrass Lady Tremaine in any way. There were whispers, wherever she went, but so far Lady Tremaine had been proven correct in her assumption that the *ton* would be too polite to ever say anything to her face.

But tonight was to be the biggest test she had been made to face so far, and Lady Tremaine said it was all the proof that Anna should need to prove that she had indeed managed to make her way into Society and to be accepted at its very highest levels. Lady Tremaine had managed to procure a voucher for them to attend Almack's, the most exclusive venue in London. It was a favored spot for members of the *ton,* and many of the people that had attended Lady Tremaine's Christmas Eve ball would be there. Anna would be expected to dance, to make small-talk, and go into supper. It would test every bit of her learning, and Anna couldn't help being more than a little bit afraid.

But even knowing how well she had faced every challenge put in her way, Anna still feared all the ways in which she could make a fool of herself at supper or out on a dance floor. She'd been so frightened as she'd arrived at the ball at the palace, especially when the Prince Regent had indeed marked her card as he'd promised earlier that day. She'd almost died when he came up to her to claim her hand and lead her through the steps. He'd been kind and complimentary of her dancing, but Anna knew she'd never been so nervous. His kindness to her, and his obvious favor had been both a blessing and a curse. Anna simply hadn't been able to imagine being able to dance and gossip and be charming all at once, the way she'd seen the young women do at Lady Tremaine's Christmas Eve ball, but it seemed she had managed to do enough to have invitations come flooding to their door ever since—and with the prince's friendship, she was even beginning to have suitors come to call. She could only pray that the Lady Patronesses of Almack's would be as similarly charmed as the Prince Regent had been.

"Miss, I have your gown ready," Mollie, Lady Tremaine's lady's maid, said as she entered Anna's room and laid the dress out on the bed. "It arrived just this morning. I've pressed it again. They never come back from the dressmaker's as good as I'd like them to be."

"Thank you, Mollie," Anna said, moving from the window to look at the gown. It was in emerald green velvet and was quite the finest thing she had ever seen. She lifted the hem and felt how soft the fabric was. "I don't deserve such finery."

"Miss, of course you do," Mollie said. "I've seen how hard you've been working to learn all the things a young lady should know. If anyone deserves to have a wonderful night in a special gown, it's you, Miss."

Anna was touched by the young woman's kindness and generosity. Many women in Mollie's position would not have been so happy for her; Anna knew that. Envy could so easily sneak into the very best of relationships, and Anna had done everything she could to try to mitigate it rearing its ugly head. She was very fond of everyone in Lady Tremaine's household. She never wanted any of the staff to think she had taken on airs and graces above her station.

"I've done nothing special, Mollie," Anna said truthfully enough. "I wasn't born to a good family. I don't even have the skills to be a scullery maid, let alone a lady's maid like you. What have I ever done that means I should be elevated so? I am constantly amazed that I'm not despised by everyone here, jumped-up little strumpet that I am."

Mollie thought about the questions Anna had asked for a moment. Her eyebrows furrowed, and her lips pursed as she did so. "You have been the companion her Ladyship wanted," she said finally. "You make her laugh. She enjoys the way you think. And you have had to turn yourself inside and out to fit in, Miss. You've worked hard, and you deserve whatever good things can come out of it. We all see it. And you have the kindest heart. Nobody could ever dislike you, Miss."

"Even that drives me crazy," Anna said sinking onto the bed beside the gown, taking care not to rumple it. "That everyone now calls me Miss or Miss Campbell. I'm just Anna. I'm no better than any of you—worse than all of you, if truth be told."

"My Ma always used to say that nobody's better than anyone else. Some just think they are," Mollie said wisely. "We're all blessed here. We work for the kindest and most generous woman in the kingdom. We all want you to do well. You're one of us, Miss."

"Anna, please, call me Anna. I don't think I can bear all the formalities a moment longer."

"Anna," Mollie said with a grin. "I shall tell everyone

else the same, but we'll have to stick with Miss when there's other's around." Anna nodded, knowing she was right. "Now, are we going to get you bathed and dressed? I've some ideas on how we can do your hair to make your lovely cheekbones and those eyes truly shine."

Anna gave a half-hearted chuckle. "Why ever not?" she said. "I may as well not look like myself, too."

Some hours later, Anna descended the stairs clad in the beautiful gown, her hair pinned in an elaborate coil of braids and curls, with matching snakes writhing in her belly. Mollie had put rouge on her cheeks to try to hide how pale she had grown, and when she looked at herself in the mirror, Anna had not recognized herself. She looked just like the ladies she'd seen at the Christmas Eve ball. But there was something else. She looked just like her mother. It had shaken Anna for a moment, to see Ma's beautiful face peering back at her, but it had given her heart. At least there was still a part of the old Anna, a bit of where she had come from, still there under all the finery.

"Oh, my!" Lady Tremaine gasped as she looked up to see her creation descending the grand staircase. "You look quite lovely."

"Thank you," Anna said, accepting the older woman's kiss to her cheek. "I cannot tell you how grateful I am for everything." She meant it. It was hard, trying to become something she wasn't, but Anna would not have ever traded places with the girl she had once been, tramping along cold, wet roads with no future, for the woman she was becoming. She had been blessed by God the day she had fallen in that ditch and broken her leg. Lady Tremaine and Lord Westerham's intervention in her life had changed everything. She may not have even survived had they not stopped and rescued her.

It was clear that such things were also on the mind of her benefactor. "And you do not ever need to do so," Lady Tremaine assured her. "I think of you as the daughter I never had. I have loved every minute of your being here. I do not know what I would do without you. I was so blessed that dear Edward spotted you lying in the road. Just think how lonely I would be if we had not found you?"

Her words were heartfelt and touched Anna deeply. "You truly are too kind," she said in a choked voice as she tried to hold back tears that seemed to have come out of nowhere.

"Now, are you ready to see how far you have come?" Lady Tremaine said, tucking her arm through Anna's and leading her towards the door. "I am so very proud of you, and you are going to be the belle of the ball tonight, I am sure of it."

Anna didn't wish to be the belle of any ball. She would be quite happy with just being noticed enough to dance a couple of reels and to perhaps make some friends. She did not wish to risk anyone's jealousy or their passion. She got into the carriage after Lady Tremaine and gazed out of the window as they traveled through the streets of London to the doors of the famous meeting place. A great number of carriages were queued up outside, waiting to drop off their inhabitants. Anna watched as lords and ladies, dukes and duchesses, and all manner of members of *the Ton* descended and entered the hallowed halls.

As their coach drew up beside the steps and a liveried doorman opened the door, Anna felt her stomach tie itself in a thousand knots. She was not ready. She'd never be ready. She was just a ragtag girl who belonged in the gutter where Lady Tremaine had found her. She did not belong here, amongst the fashionable, the wealthy and the powerful. "I can't," she whispered."

"Sorry, my dear? Did you say something?" Lady Tremaine asked as she got up to follow Anna out of the carriage.

Anna stood in the open doorway. "I can't go in there," she said. "This is not who I am. I'll never fit in here. Everyone will know and will hate me for trying to be something I am not."

"Nonsense. None of them have the first idea about real breeding," Lady Tremaine said dismissively. "Anyway, what do you care what any of those snobs think? The Prince Regent and Queen Charlotte have both given you their patronage and favor. You need not fear anyone here."

"But I do not wish to embarrass you," Anna wailed.

"You'll never do that. I couldn't care one bit what they think of me, so I'm certainly not going to bother myself with what they think of you."

"If you don't care for them, then why are we here?"

"Because I want you to have some fun. From everything you've told me about your life, you've never had so much as an ounce of the damn stuff. I want you to know what being a young girl should be—before you aren't one anymore." Lady Tremaine put an arm around Anna's waist. "You are better than any one of them." She nodded towards the string of people entering Almack's. "And you need not ever fear their opinion of you. I know precisely who you are."

Her words were comforting, but Anna's belly did not settle down. They got out of the coach and began to climb the steps. They were about to enter when Lord Edward bounded up behind them. "You came," he said delightedly. He smiled at them both and kissed his godmother on the cheek before he took Anna's hand and kissed the back of it. His touch made her body sing, and she was not lost to the fact he had actually pressed his lips to her skin—not just kissed the air above it, as was more proper.

He offered each of them an arm. "Don't you both look lovely," he said as they tucked their arms through his and allowed him to escort them inside. "Now, I believe I made you a promise, Miss Campbell, that I would be the first man to mark your card. I should very much like to do just that, as soon as we get inside."

"Thank you, Edward," Lady Tremaine said fondly.

"There is no need," Anna said. "You don't have to if you don't want to. You made that promise a long time ago."

"Not want to!" Edward exclaimed. "Have you not looked around you, Miss Campbell? You are quite the loveliest young lady here. I would be a fool not to want to dance with you."

Anna blushed at his effusive compliment. He truly was the kindest of men. She had prayed he would be at the Prince's ball, the night of her Coming Out, but though it was clear that he was a part of Prinny's inner circle of friends, he had not attended. Anna was most glad to see him here tonight, and she smiled as he took up her dance card from the table near the door and busily scribbled his name against a number of the dances. He grinned at her as he finished doing so with a flourish. "I have claimed the dances before and after supper, so I might escort you into the dining room," he said as though it was quite the most normal thing in the world. "Oh, and the last dance, too, so I might escort you and dear Lady Frances home. You don't mind, do you?"

Anna smiled shyly as he handed it to her. "You are too kind to me," she said softly.

"Nonsense," he admonished her. "I shall have quite the best companion to talk to at supper—and shall have the pleasure of at least three dances where my feet will not be trodden on."

Anna giggled. She'd inflicted him with more than his fair share of hurts as he'd patiently taken her through the steps. He always made light of it, and never seemed to mind when she went left when she should go right, or forward when she should go back. "I shall try my very hardest to give your poor feet some respite." She knew that what she was saying, and how she was saying it, might be construed as flirtatious.

Her tone was light, but the way he held her gaze and the manner in which he smiled at her made Anna feel most discomfited. She looked down at her own feet and took a deep breath. When she looked up again, he was no longer gazing at her with those wide blue eyes of his. He was looking out over the heads of the attendees, clearly looking to see who was there. "If you will excuse me, ladies," he said politely when he finally looked back at Anna and Lady Frances, "I see a gentleman that I must speak with. I shall leave you both to enjoy your evening—and shall come and find you when it is time for me to claim your hand, Miss Campbell." He bowed to them both, then disappeared off into the crowds.

"He is the sweetest boy," Lady Tremaine said, pulling out a feathered fan and wafting it in front of her face. "Now, I shall find myself somewhere to sit so I may watch over the proceedings. Will you accompany me, my dear? Your sharp eyes may spot those I'd like to spend my evening with—and those I'd rather avoid."

"Of course, your ladyship," Anna said, but Lady Tremaine had already set off in search of friends and foes. Anna trailed behind her, smiling politely as they stopped from time to time, so Lady Tremaine might introduce her to someone or another.

As they made their way to the side of the ballroom, Anna spied the tall, slender frame of Viscount Comey on the other side of the dance floor. He was accompanying a thin girl with a long face. He looked solemn, his lips moving surreptitiously as he tried to recall the steps, no doubt. Anna nodded towards him, "Lady Tremaine, your great-nephew is here."

Lady Tremaine glanced over at him. "Oh, drat," she said, rolling her eyes and pulling a face. "Of all the people in London."

CHAPTER TEN

Anna couldn't help but agree with her employer's exclamation. Viscount Comey had fast become one of her least favorite people, and like Lady Tremaine, she had been glad that they had managed to avoid his company for much of the time they had been in London. There was too much about him that seemed untrustworthy. The way he spoke to the other servants at Trelawney Hall, as if they had nothing better to do than to be at his beck and call, and he never asked for anything nicely—nor did he ever say thank you. "Would you like to go?" Anna asked her employer a little hopefully. Her nerves were already on the raw; that Viscount Comey might be here and see her fail would be just too much to bear.

"No, we can't let that little toad think he has us rattled," Lady Tremaine said. "I know you think he would delight in seeing you get something wrong—and you are right, he probably would—but you won't make any errors. You just need to be yourself. And know this, my dear: you are twice as bright as he will ever be. I'd wager you could put him in his place in a heartbeat—so don't be intimidated by him."

"I shall do my best to ignore him completely," Anna assured her, though it seemed that Viscount Comey had now seen them. He was hurriedly crossing the dance floor, his companion trailing miserably behind him, and seemed to be headed right for the spot where Lady Tremaine and Anna were standing.

Lady Tremaine raised her eyes to the heavens and tutted loudly. "I suppose we shall have to be polite," she said, taking one of the seats nearby. She sat in it as though it were a throne, and she was holding court. Anna couldn't help but admire her aplomb.

Viscount Comey bowed deeply to his aunt. "Dear Great-Aunt Frances, I am delighted to see you here," he said obsequiously whilst he also contrived to completely ignore Anna's presence at all.

"I'm sure you are," Lady Tremaine said drily. "Have you forgotten the manners you were raised with?" she asked with an arched eyebrow as she looked first at Anna and then at Viscount Comey's companion who was standing a few steps behind him, looking petrified.

Viscount Comey looked blank for a moment, then looked where his aunt's eyes were going. "Oh, of course. Good evening, Miss Campbell. You look quite lovely." His tone was petulant like a little boy forced to make an apology for something he had done and did not wish to admit to. "Please, may I introduce you to Lady Jane Fairley?" The young woman stepped forward and curtsied to Lady Tremaine, then nodded towards Anna.

"Your father is Earl Robert Fairley?" Lady Tremaine

asked the girl, who nodded. She was too frightened to speak. "A good man. Fine estate in Hampshire, if I remember rightly?" The girl nodded again but did not speak a word.

"Lady Jane is to become my wife," Viscount Comey said. "She is her father's sole heir, the entail upon her estate is much like our own." He took her hand in his, his expression proprietary as if he were marking her as his territory. Lady Jane squirmed a little but did not pull away. The words he'd just uttered should have been said with love and pride, and should not ever have been uttered alongside the mercenary comment about a favorable entail attached. He should have been gazing down at his affianced with at least some smidgeon of affection—but Viscount Comey was looking at his fiancée with a disdainful expression, and the way in which Lady Jane flinched at his words, and at his touch, told Anna that she wasn't too enamored of the situation either.

The news that this poor girl had a fine inheritance was probably the only reason he was prepared to wed a woman he clearly did not much like, and certainly held little respect for, Anna thought to herself. He truly was just like her Pa, always looking out for whatever little trick might get him more of what he wished for. Poor Lady Jane looked like she would rather die than be stood beside him, much less marry him. She didn't like Viscount Comey, and she knew full well that as soon as Lady Tremaine passed away and he took possession of his inheritance, she would be back on the streets. The thought made her a little reckless. She could sow a little discord here so very easily.

"Lady Jane, should you like to come up to the gallery to meet with some of my friends?" she asked kindly. She may despise Viscount Comey—and if her reading of the situation was correct, so did Lady Jane—but this young woman deserved to be taken on her merits. That she seemed to be so uncomfortable around Viscount Comey only made Anna sure that she and Lady Tremaine would probably warm to this young woman in no time. Anna turned to Lady Tremaine, who gave her a look of sincere approval.

"Lady Aster is here, and Mary Cordwainer, if your Ladyship can spare me?" Anna asked, adhering to the rules that applied to her as merely a lady's companion, so Viscount Comey could not possibly accuse her of over-stepping her bounds. The young woman's eyes lit up, clearly delighted that she might be able to escape from Viscount Comey's clutches for at least a few minutes.

"I think that a splendid idea," Lady Tremaine said with a wicked glint in her eye, seeing exactly Anna's intentions, and obviously approving of them. Viscount Comey gave Anna an angry look but did not dare to be impolite in such a public space.

"Would you mind?" Lady Jane asked him, her eyes full of hope.

"Not at all," Viscount Comey said through gritted teeth, knowing that to some extent, he had been outma-neuvered, though he might not know in what way it might come back to harm him. "It will give you the chance to meet some of the people you'll be making company with once..." he trailed off. Even he was not so callous as to mention his great-aunt's passing in such a way. Lady Jane gasped at his indiscretion, but nobody else was surprised by it.

"Once I am dead, my dear, is what my great-nephew meant to say," Lady Tremaine said bluntly to Lady Jane. "I am only of use to him because he will inherit my estate. But that is quite alright, as he is of no use at all to me." With that, Viscount Comey was dismissed. His face went puce with rage he could not express. He turned on his heel and stormed away through the crowds.

Anna and Lady Tremaine grinned at one another. "Please do forgive us," Lady Tremaine said, turning to Lady Jane. "But you must be aware of what a dreadful bore he can be?"

"I am. I have begged my father to marry me to anyone else," Lady Jane said, then slapped a hand to her mouth, knowing she had said too much.

"You do not ever need to be tactful with me," Lady Tremaine said, reaching out to pull Lady Jane's hand away from her face. "Don't be ashamed of not liking someone. And never give up the hope that there may be an alternative. Now, you and Anna should go and have some fun with people your age. It is a pleasure to meet you, Lady Jane."

Anna led the young woman through the crowds and climbed the stairs up to the gallery. A small group of young women stood peering over the edge at those dancing and talking below them. Anna greeted them warmly. All of them had become good friends in the months of being in London. None of them had ever judged her for her less than stellar bloodlines—and for that, she would always be loyal to them. Anna quickly introduced them all to Lady Jane, and soon they had enveloped the scared young woman with their gossip and their friendship. From time to time, one or another of them would disappear to dance with some young man; sometimes they were all claimed at once. Anna had been surprised that so many young men had asked for a dance with her, and she was quite fagged by the time the dance before supper came around.

Lord Westerham tapped the shoulder of her partner, and they bowed to one another. Anna curtsied to Lord Westerham, who then bowed to her, then held out his hand so she might lay hers lightly upon it. Anna had been enjoying the dancing until now. She had forgotten that only a few short months earlier, she had not known the steps to a single one of the reels she had just performed and had barely been able to stand on her own two feet. But suddenly, her new-found confidence in her skill vanished as she looked up into the eyes of the man beside her; the snakes in her belly that had finally grown dormant now began their interminable writhing once more. She wished that he did not make her feel so peculiar when he was near, yet for some reason, he did.

He smiled warmly at her as the music began. "I've been watching you," he said. "You truly are one of the finest dancers here tonight. You should be very proud of how much you have learned."

"Thank you," Anna said. Her chest was tight, her mouth dry, though her palms felt unbearably sweaty. Being so close to Lord Westerham in front of all eyes seemed so much more intimate than their lessons in the library had ever been. He was by far the most handsome man in the room, and there was an aura around him of confidence that made him even more compelling. Anna had been more than half in love with him in the confines of Lady Tremaine's townhouse. Here at Almack's, he was fast taking on the attributes of the Greek Gods that her benefactress had been teaching her about.

The music started, and they began to follow the calls of the dancing master. Anna tried to pay attention to his voice, to focus on anything other than Lord Westerham's light touches on her hands or her waist. She could feel the warmth of his skin and the strength of the muscles in his arms as he lifted her when told to do so. He did so as if she weighed less than a feather. She felt safe, yet she also felt utterly at sea and could not make sense of such contradictory sensations. Her body felt afire, tingling from top to toe whilst her head was fuzzy and disordered in a way that she was most unused to.

"So, how are you finding Society, Miss Campbell?" Lord Westerham asked her as they moved towards one another, then began a promenade step through their set.

It seemed such a simple question to ask and required nothing more than a simple answer, yet Anna struggled to speak. She didn't know what to say. She didn't know if Lord Westerham was just being polite, or if his flirtatious tone and amused eyes meant something more than this being just a dance. He was such a genial man with a manner that was capable of making everyone around him feel wanted and appreciated. There was no reason why he would treat her in a manner that was different from anybody else here, yet he seemed to be doing just that. She had not seen him smile the way he was at her to any other girl tonight. She'd not heard or seen him seem so interested in the answers that his gentle question might elicit. She was so confused.

Everything about this polite and mannered world made understanding others so very difficult. It made her miss the simple straightforwardness of her life before. Life may have been hard, but you always knew if someone liked you or not. People in her old life had always spoken their minds. They did not say nice things to people when they wished to say unpleasant ones. Men did not dance with girls that they didn't find attractive. This world Anna now found herself a part of had more in almost every sense, but they most certainly did not have the peace of mind that simple truth could bring.

"I find it mostly quite congenial, my Lord," she said, trying hard to continue to focus upon the steps. She did not wish to miss one, to catch her foot in her gown and to fall again. She was still a little unsteady on her feet, though her leg had healed very well. She did not wish to embarrass Lord Westerham or disgrace Lady Tremaine. She lived in fear of people finding out who she truly was, though it seemed that whilst she had Lady Tremaine's patronage, there was nobody here that would ever ask her about it to her face. Such things simply weren't discussed —at least not until people were amongst their close circles, when gossip about those not favored by them could be talked of in confidence.

Her eyes caught upon Viscount Comey and Lady Jane. Lady Tremaine's nephew was just one such member of the *ton*. He, no doubt, spent much time insulting Anna and his great-aunt when neither they nor any of their friends were present to defend themselves. He glared at her from across the chamber, and his masked venom made Anna shiver. "Though there are some present tonight that I'd rather I'd never met," she added in a low voice that only Lord Westerham would have been able to hear.

Lord Westerham followed her eyes then chuckled. "He is a dreadful bore."

"I fear he may be much worse than that," Anna admitted. "There is something about him that quite simply makes my skin crawl. I've seen him in huddles with one of the valets when he visits his great-aunt, and they always seem to break apart as soon as they realize I am there. I fear he is up to no good."

"He does have a slimy nature," Lord Westerham said. "I must confess, I have never liked him, not even when we were boys together at school."

Anna nodded, glad that he agreed with her. "I hate that he will be the one to inherit everything Lady Tremaine holds so dear. He will ruin it, will run it all into the ground before she has even settled in her grave. He is not just untrustworthy. I do not know what it is about him, but he is not what he seems—of that I am sure."

"Thankfully, our dear friend is not at death's door just yet," Lord Westerham said. "Though do you still retire to Bath next week?"

"We do," Anna said a little sadly. It wasn't that she would miss all the hullabaloo of life in London, but she would miss her friends, and would especially miss this kind and handsome man who was smiling at her so warmly as they danced.

"Is Viscount Comey to join you?" Lord Westerham asked.

Anna was slightly puzzled by his interest in the matter. "I don't think so, though I am sure he will bless us with a visit from time to time," she added drily. "I wish he wouldn't. He always makes me think that he is up to something, or at the very least keeping something from Lady Tremaine."

"Should you like me to look into him, to see if there is anything he is doing that he should not?"

"I should have thought that, given your affection for Lady Tremaine, you would wish to do such a thing without my asking it of you," Anna said a little pointedly, though she immediately regretted the harshness of her tone when he looked so stung by her words.

"You are, of course, quite right," he said with a rueful laugh. "I accept your reprimand; it is well deserved. I shall do all I can and shall let you know of my findings should anything be found."

The dance came to an end, and all the couples around them began to leave the dance floor and head towards the doors and cross the hall to the dining room. Lord Westerham held her hand where it rested upon his arm. "You need not fear; they all have dreadful table manners," he said with a smile. "And the food here is notorious for being unpalatable, so you'll not want to touch it—whichever fork you think might be the correct one."

"Is my fear so easy to see? I had thought I was doing a fine job of fitting in." Anna tried to make her tone sound light as if such things didn't matter to her at all.

"And you have melded into this world admirably," Lord Westerham said, obviously proud of her for doing so. "Nobody would know. It isn't obvious—not to anyone else. But I have spent considerably more time with you, so I know your little mannerisms. Your body gets tight and stiff when you are anxious; you cock your head slightly to the left and your eyes barely blink."

Anna was aghast at the thought that he should know her so well. She had not noticed him taking such close notice of her—and she did not like it that he had been so very observant. It implied that he had been watching her every move and that in itself only served to make her anxiety greater. She could only hope that he had not realized that she was, in truth, far more nervous about being so close to him as she was right now, rather than being afraid of the busy supper-room.

Now was not the time to discuss such things though —nor even to think upon them as they were soon jostled into their places and supper was being served. She took her seat, finding an eighteen-year-old viscount seated to her left, while Lord Westerham took the seat to her right. Anna was delighted to see that her friend, Mary Cordwainer, was seated opposite them. She had been escorted into supper by her fiancé, Captain Elliot Winters. Her beaming smile made Anna very happy. She winked at her friend, and Mary grinned back.

"Your friend seems unusually delighted, given the quality of the fare," Lord Westerham said as the soup was served to them.

"I think she is forcing her jollity. She has had most bittersweet news today. She and Captain Winters are to be wed on Saturday. They have a special dispensation from his regiment," Anna said quietly. "He is to go to Portugal to serve under Wellesley in just over a week's time. I am glad that she will know that she is his and will have some happy memories to keep her company whilst he is gone away."

"I am sure he will be glad of recollections of his lovely bride, too," Lord Westerham said, his words heavy with meaning. "It is a hard life, that of a soldier—especially given the dangers ahead of him on the Peninsular."

"Is it as dreadful as the newspapers say?" Anna asked.

"I've not been myself, but I have friends who have served King and Country. All of them bear the scars."

"Would you ever go?

"I would not wish to, but if it were my duty to do so, then, of course, I would go," Lord Westerham said thoughtfully. "I do not think that war is the answer to many things if I am truly honest, but I serve my King. I serve my country. I would do what was expected of me."

Anna admired him for his honesty. It seemed to her that too few men considered whether fighting endless wars was a suitable manner to bring about change. Anna had seen many fights in her short life, yet she had never known any of them to solve the issue that had purportedly been their cause. Men, it seemed to her, simply wanted a reason to be angry and to express that anger through violent means. She already admired Lord Westerham more than she should, but his considered answer on such a matter raised him ever higher in her estimations. "You are an interesting man, my Lord," Anna told him.

"I am hoping that is a compliment," Lord Westerham said, his eyes not leaving hers, his smile warm. He slipped his hand over hers, and Anna felt a frisson of sensation course through her body at this gentle touch.

"It is," she admitted, unable to tear her eyes or her hand away. She knew she should not feel this way about him, but it had crept up on her over these many weeks, and now she did not know how to turn it off. She had fallen in love with him, quite against her wishes, and now she didn't know how to stop loving him.

CHAPTER ELEVEN

L ondon seemed dull without Miss Campbell in it, Edward thought as he made his way along Pall Mall and entered his club. She had only been gone for two days, and already he missed her terribly. She had crept into his mind and his heart, though there was little he could do about it. His father would never agree to such a match, no matter how much Edward begged him to understand—of that, Edward was certain. But he had made her a promise—and by finding out about what Comey might be up to, he would be serving Prinny, too.

Because of the Prince Regent's intervention in the matter, Edward already knew that Comey had been called out by the father of a young woman that he'd attempted to seduce. Natalia Coraline had believed that he intended to marry her—but when she'd seen the announcement of Comey's engagement to Lady Jane Fairley, she'd known that he'd been leading her a merry dance and had been forced to tell her father that she was regrettably in the family way. Boris Coraline, a half-

Russian merchant with a reputation for having a foul temper and perfect aim, had not taken the news well. If it weren't for Edward's intervention, Coraline would have shot Comey dead in their duel, of that Edward had few doubts.

That matter dealt with, he'd hoped that Comey might have had the good sense to keep his nose out of mischief —at least for a little while—but it seemed that he was attracted to trouble the way a moth is lured to a flame. Edward had already found out about the man's gambling debts amongst their peers, and the many promises he'd made and broken in regard to making good on those debts. Comey was not a man to be trusted; that was something that almost everyone who knew him could agree upon.

But there were also hints that Comey had gotten himself mixed up in something altogether more danger- ous, and Edward hoped that his old friend, Jonathan Winston, might be able to help him find out more. As he handed over his hat and coat to the doorman, he could see his old friend already seated in one of the high-backed leather chairs by the fire, nursing a brandy. Winston was a wiry man with a neatly trimmed beard and eagle-sharp eyes. He missed nothing and was one of the cleverest men Edward had ever known. If anyone could find out the information that Edward needed, it would be him.

Edward approached Winston quickly. His old friend stood up, and they shook hands firmly. Winston looked anxious, and that immediately set Edward on edge. "You've found something?" he asked as they took their seats. Winston signaled to one of the footmen that he should bring them both another drink, then turned to look Edward straight in the eye.

"This Comey fellow is about as rotten as they come," he said bluntly. "Westerham, I do hope he's no friend of yours."

"Not a friend," Edward admitted, "but he is the great-nephew of my godmother. Will what he's doing impact her in any way?"

"I'd be surprised if it didn't," Winston said. "Let me start with his recent disagreement with Coraline." Edward nodded and leaned forward in his seat. "You managed to stop the duel; do you mind me asking how you managed that? Boris Coraline is not known for stepping away from a fight, and he always does whatever he has to do to win."

"Coraline was naturally concerned for his daughter's reputation. I arranged for her to go and stay at my family estate until the child is due and arranged a marriage between Miss Natalia and my father's bailiff. Her good name is preserved, and it meant Coraline was in my debt. I asked that he back out of the duel before it became public knowledge."

"I can see how that would have appeased Coraline, at least for a time," Winston said, nodding his head. "How did you know that there was a duel to be fought?"

"Prinny told me," Edward said. He had no doubt that Winston would keep their conversation to himself, so felt no fear in revealing it. "He wanted it stopped, though he did not say why. He made out that it was simply because he was concerned for Lady Tremaine should such a thing come out in public."

"Interesting," Winston said, scratching at his beard. "I know everyone says Prinny is a bit of a fool, but he is invariably on top of things before almost anyone else."

Edward smiled at that. He'd always thought that Prinny's outward appearance as a loveable, but ultimately foolish, man was nothing more than a façade. He'd always found the prince to be quick-witted and sharp as a tack on every subject that was ever discussed around him.

"What is there to know, Winston?"

"Viscount Comey is in debt."

"I know that. Everyone in town carries his letters."

"Not just gambling debts amongst the *ton*," Winston said, his face solemn. "He owes money to all manner of people. People like Coraline—and worse. He's mortgaged his own estate to the hilt—even though he does not come of age for another six years according to the entail upon his father's estate—and if he defaults on the payment due this quarter, he will lose everything. You can imagine the kinds of men willing to make loans upon an estate not held entire?" Edward nodded sadly. Comey had ever been a fool, but to take such risks with all he had seemed ill-thought-out at best, and idiotic to him.

"It will most likely be the debtors' prison for him," Winston went on. "It is why he is so determined to make a suitable match. I think he'd once hoped that by marrying Natalia Coraline, he'd gain Boris' allegiance. It would have been a sensible thing for him to do. Coraline is respected and feared in good circles and bad. He'd have paid off Comey's debts, and probably have set the couple up with a comfortable allowance."

"So why would he then move his attentions to Lady Fairley?"

"Because Lady Jane has something Natalia Coraline does not have," Winston said. "She is a member of Society. Coraline would never be accepted in a club like this, much less be able to get his daughter presented at Court. I think Comey saw the opportunity to wed Lady Jane as the way out of all his troubles. Her dowry is substantial, and even if it wasn't, she stands to inherit everything from her father, which would mean that Comey would become an Earl, a title over and above his own current rank—and would gain a far greater estate than that of Lady Tremaine—and Fairley is known to be sick and at death's door. Everything would be in Comey's grasp if he could survive until then."

"He realized that by taking Miss Coraline, he would always be indebted to her father—who I can assure you is hale and hearty and has no intention of dying to please anyone," Edward said, seeing precisely why a marriage to the biddable Lady Jane would be so much more appealing to Comey than a match with the fiery Russian's daughter. "He'd always be a supplicant, never in control of his own life. Being an Earl, rather than a mere Viscount would also appeal to his dreadful vanity."

"But rumor has it that his biddable little bride is having second thoughts," Winston said. "I have heard whispers that since she met your Lady Tremaine and her companion..."

"Miss Campbell," Edward said, wishing she were still here and could hear what Winston was telling him.

"Indeed, Miss Campbell," Winston said, a flicker of

amusement playing over his watchful eyes as he noted Edward's reaction to her name. "It seems that Comey's docile bride has become considerably less so. She is refusing to let her father set a date for the nuptials, and I am told that Comey is furious."

"Do you think he will do something to Lady Jane?"

Winston paused as if he were weighing how to say what needed to be said. "No, I don't. I think he'll be glad to be rid of her. But I do fear for Miss Campbell and Lady Tremaine."

"But why?" Edward felt a pang of fear. He did not want to believe such a thing—though he knew that a cornered rat would always attack, and Comey had somehow trapped himself in the tightest of spaces. "I know he is a rotter, but he's always seemed to care—in his own peculiar way—for his great-aunt, and Miss Campbell is nothing to him."

"On the contrary," Winston said. "She has, unwittingly or otherwise, ruined his prospects of marriage to Lady Jane. She has the ear of his great-aunt, and I am told Lady Tremaine is most fond of her indeed. Comey would be quite justified in fearing that she may seek to change the entail on her estate and leave all to Miss Campbell."

"But she wouldn't, and even if she did, Miss Campbell would not accept it. She simply isn't that type of woman."

"Are you sure of that?" Winston asked. "Where did she come from? Nobody knows anything about her. Her life before coming to London for the Season is a mystery to everyone—including you, my friend. How do you know that she did not worm her way into Lady

Tremaine's affections with just such a scheme in mind?"

"Because we picked her up off the road, at death's door," Edward exploded. "She didn't seek us out. She has never done anything to make me think that she wants money or position of any kind. She balks at every penny my godmother spends on her and even refused to be moved to one of the bedroom suites downstairs because she feels her place is amongst the servants in the attics."

"She could be a very fine actress," Winston said, his tone cautionary.

"She could, but I am sure that she is not."

"I pray you are right, because if I am right about Comey, then she is going to need to be wary of his every move. He is likely to do all he can to discredit her, to have her thrown from Lady Tremaine's household. Comey needs her gone, or he cannot gain control of Lady Tremaine—and if he is not to be wed to either Miss Natalia or Lady Jane, then he needs her gone."

Edward was surprised at how starkly Winston had just said that he thought Comey capable of doing something to harm Lady Frances. For a moment, he didn't speak. He leaned back in the chair and ran his fingers through his hair, rubbed at his cheek, then leaned forward again. "You truly think he might do something to harm Lady Frances?" he asked.

"I think he is a desperate man," Winston said softly. "If he does not find a considerable amount of money, and soon, he will be likely to lose his own life. You and I both know Comey; do you think he'd be likely to value his great-aunt's life over his own?"

Edward shook his head. He did not. Comey would never value anyone's life over his own. He would do whatever it took for him to survive, and if that meant he had to harm others along the way, it wouldn't trouble him in the slightest. "Thank you, Winston," he said. "I shall write to Miss Campbell immediately and will tell her to be on her guard. As long as she is with Lady Frances, I know my godmother will be safe."

"I hope you are right. But what if he succeeds in getting her out of the household?"

"I shall have to tell my mother, too. She is Lady Frances' oldest friend. Nobody would think anything peculiar in her going to Bath early to be with her. We will keep her safe. We have to."

The footman brought a tray with two glasses of brandy upon it and set them down in front of the two men. "I think we may need the bottle," Winston said, looking at Edward.

Edward felt cold and clammy. He was sure he must be white as a sheet having heard the information Winston had just given him. He reached for the brandy and downed first one glass and then the other in quick succession. Winston gave him a concerned look but said nothing. He'd always been good at letting a man be alone with his thoughts. He did not need to fill the air with inane gossip or small talk to break the silence. He was content with what was and let Edward come to terms with his news in his own time.

When the men parted some hours later, Edward's head was fuzzy from the brandy, and his heart filled with fear. He stumbled towards a hansom carriage and gave the driver his mother's address on Harley Street. She would scold him for his drunkenness, but he did not doubt that she would know what to do to try to keep Miss Campbell and Lady Frances safe. But he fell asleep in the carriage and woke up in his old room the next morning with a throbbing headache and a fervent hope that everything Winston had told him was just a dream. Yet he knew it was not and so he got up and padded across the chamber to his bureau. He opened it, took up a pen and a bottle of ink, reached for a sheet of paper, and began to write.

Dear Miss Campbell,

I am writing to you because I fear that you may be in some danger. I am sorry to be so blunt and to tell you this in this way, but I see no other way to warn you. I know you would rather I not bother with unnecessary platitudes and requests after your health, under the circumstances. I pray that this letter will reach you before it is too late.

You must be careful of Viscount Comey. He is in the most dire straits, and I believe that he may seek to cause you harm or have you removed from Lady Frances' household. Lady Jane Fairley is having doubts about their match and is stalling their wedding. This means he has no access to the funds he needs to pay his debts unless Lady Tremaine passes soon. You must do everything you can to resist his attempts to have you put out, or I fear the very worst may happen and he may do something dreadful to affect Lady Frances' health.

Be careful. Do not let anyone see this letter; burn it

after you have read it. I will do all I can to get to Bath swiftly to be there for you and will send my mother as soon as she can travel. Stay safe, and do not ever trust Viscount Comey; he bears you nothing but ill will.

Yours, most affectionately,
Edward

IT WAS SHORT, but Edward felt it conveyed the need for Miss Campbell to be wary. He sealed it and called for his valet. "See this is sent via the most reliable man you have. It must reach Miss Campbell's hand alone."

His valet nodded and disappeared with the note just as his mother appeared in the doorway. "How are you?" she asked pointedly, gliding across the floor and sitting in the armchair by the bed. "I had to get the stable lads in to carry you upstairs last night."

Edward gave her an apologetic look. "My head is throbbing, but you'll understand why I was in my cups, I promise," he assured her. He moved to perch on the edge of the bed and told her everything he had found out. She blanched and bit her lip.

"I cannot leave until the end of the month, at least," she said, looking at him with remorse in her eyes. "The house in Bath will need to be made ready, and all the packing here will take an age. If things are as bad as you think they may be, will that be too late?"

"We shall have to pray it is not. I am sure Miss Campbell will find a way to keep her place. Lady Frances values her more highly than she does Viscount Comey, of that I am sure—but he is a wily one, and I don't doubt that he will make life very difficult for her indeed."

"Then it is as well that she has been warned," Mama said. "But we must do all you can to help her to protect my dearest friend. I could not bear to lose either of them."

CHAPTER TWELVE

Bath was quite lovely, Anna thought as she got up and looked out of the window of her third new room in a little over six months. Lady Tremaine's friends, Viscount Kingston and his kindly wife, were lovely and had made them very welcome to their grand house on the Royal Crescent. Anna had not seen very much of the viscount since they arrived as he split his time between London and Bath, attending parliament, but he was due to return very soon when Parliament went into recess over the summer.

Viscountess Kingston, Lady Matilda as she had urged Anna to call her, was some ten years younger than her husband and Lady Tremaine. She was witty and urbane, wore only the most current of fashions, and apparently had a lot of influence in local politics, which fascinated Anna. She was not used to women like Lady Matilda at all, though they had become fast friends in no time. Lady Matilda had been delighted to continue Anna's education in the fine art of becoming a lady, and she insisted that Anna accompany her everywhere.

Each morning, they went took a long walk together in the park, whilst Lady Tremaine took the waters, and Lady Matilda explained the intricacies of politics and the war in the Peninsular, who Anna would most need to impress, and who she need not concern herself with. It was an education that would change Anna in many ways. She grew in confidence under the clever tutelage of her hostess, and so when Viscount Comey had arrived last night, without having announced his intention to do so as usual, Anna was much better equipped to deal with his snide comments and rude behavior.

Washing and dressing without any fuss, Anna gave her reflection in the cheval glass a quick check before she made her way downstairs for breakfast. Viscount Comey was already in the dining room. He was standing with his back to the door. His shoulders were held tightly, his hands were clenched in fists by his sides, and as Anna drew closer, she could hear Lady Tremaine remonstrating with him about his dreadful manners.

"You should have written to me," she said firmly. "It is all well and good, you're doing things such as this when I am staying in one of my own homes—but here, I am a guest. My welcome will soon be quite worn out with the viscountess if she is expected to put up my guests without so much as a by your leave."

"I am sorry, Aunt," he said, his tone clipped. "You are, of course, right. I shall ensure I announce my intentions to visit with you in good time in the future."

Anna could tell that he didn't mean a word of it. He

liked the way his unexpected visits threw a house into turmoil. He wanted to create chaos and ill-feeling; he seemed to thrive upon it. She wondered why but knew she would never understand a man like Viscount Comey —and nor did she wish to do so.

She cleared her throat politely, announcing her arrival as she entered the dining room. Viscount Comey turned and gave her a perfunctory greeting. Lady Tremaine smiled as though she were relieved to be no longer alone with her great-nephew. He truly made everyone around him feel on edge—and even Lady Tremaine, who was usually so composed, was not immune to the way in which he transformed the mood.

"Good morning, Miss Campbell," Viscount Comey said through gritted teeth.

"And to you, Viscount Comey," Anna said politely, bobbing a curtsey to them both. She moved to the breakfast buffet and began to help herself to bacon and scrambled eggs from the silver servers on the sideboard. "May I fetch you anything, Lady Tremaine?"

"Just some chocolate, my dear," Lady Tremaine said, sounding a little weary again.

The countess had been feeling so much better since they had left London, and Anna had been glad to see her so full of vitality once more. It seemed obvious that much of her exhaustion in London had been due to the almost constant presence of her great-nephew, and that was sad, Anna thought. Her family had not been perfect, but even when Pa had been at his worst, he'd never meant to hurt her in any way. Even when he'd beaten her he'd never taken a belt or a stick to her as so many men would, and had always been dreadfully sorry when he sobered up and realized what he had done. It was all too clear that Viscount Comey's intention, wherever he went, was to cause as much disruption and unpleasantness as he could.

"Are you quite well? If you wish, I could arrange for your carriage to be brought around later today, perhaps after lunch, to take you to the baths?"

"No, though thank you for thinking of me," Lady Tremaine said. "I shall keep with my routine. We are to attend Lady Hartley's at home this afternoon, remember?" Viscount Comey looked up at the name. Anna was sure she saw his eyes narrow a little, but as soon as he was aware that she had seen him, he gave her a disingenuous smile. It made Anna's stomach turn.

"Of course we are," Anna said, suddenly feeling a little weary herself. The Hartleys were very kind, but their two young daughters had taken a liking to Anna and followed her everywhere like well-trained pups. It was flattering and sweet, but Anna found the girls to be rude and spiteful if she did not do everything they wished her to. That she now also had to keep a close eye on Viscount Comey, too, seemed more than she could bear in a single day.

Viscount Comey moved to stand beside Anna at the sideboard as she began to pour the steaming hot chocolate for herself and Lady Tremaine. "These Hartley's you speak of, are they the Hartley's involved in the sugar trade?"

"I don't know," Anna said thoughtfully. "Mr. Hartley

has a shipping company, based out of Bristol I think, but what they trade in I do not know"

"Ah, then they are the family I am thinking of. Hartley sugar is quite renowned," Viscount Comey said, his voice a little pompous. He was clearly delighted by the news that the Hartley's were a part of his great-aunt's social circle here in Bath. "Do they have a daughter called Amelia?"

"No, but I believe they have a niece," Anna replied. "Why would you ask, my Lord?"

"Nothing in particular," he said, trying to sound nonchalant as he heaped spoonfuls of the buttery eggs onto a plate for himself. Anna was not fooled; there was clearly something important about this Amelia Hartley. She wondered if Viscount Comey was hoping to make a new match, given that his engagement with Lady Jane Fairley seemed to have come to an end, according to Lady Tremaine.

"I shall accompany you, Aunt," he informed Lady Tremaine, "to the Hartleys so that I might introduce myself to your friends."

"I am sure they will be delighted," Lady Tremaine said drily.

Anna watched Viscount Comey closely as he ate his breakfast, drank his coffee, and then stood up to leave the dining room. He took huge mouthfuls and often spoke with his mouth full, willfully ignoring all the rules of eating in polite society that Lady Tremaine, Lord Westerham, and Lady Matilda had taught her—but she had the strongest suspicion that he was doing so on purpose. She did not know if he was trying to shame her, or if he was simply making a joke in the poorest of taste, but it did not endear him to her in any way. The more she knew of him, the less she wished to be near him at all.

"Miss Campbell, would you perhaps like to join me for a short walk whilst my aunt takes the waters?" Viscount Comey asked her unexpectedly.

Anna was taken aback. Her immediate reaction was to refuse him. She would never wish to spend time with Viscount Comey unless it was necessary. But she knew that would be impolite, so she was delighted when Lady Matilda swept into the dining room. "I'm afraid that won't be possible, Viscount Comey," she said airily. "Miss Campbell is to accompany me to the seamstress this morning. Our new gowns are ready, though they will need a final fitting to be sure. We will be gone all morning."

"Another time, then, perhaps?" Viscount Comey said, his tone oddly gentle.

"Of course," Anna assured him, though she prayed that there would be sufficient excuses to prevent such a thing from ever happening. He'd never much noticed her before, and his doing so now was somewhat unsettling.

Once he'd left the chamber and they'd heard him tell the butler to have his horse brought around so he might take a ride in the park, the women all grinned at one another. "I am so sorry he has descended upon you without so much as a word," Lady Tremaine said sadly. "He never thinks and is so rude sometimes. I can forgive many things, but never a liar and he is sadly so mired in untruths as to actually believe the nonsense he has created in his own mind."

"Nonsense, who amongst us does not have a dreadful relative tucked away somewhere," Lady Matilda said with a chuckle. "I know that I do—and you have yet to meet Harold's niece, Helena. Now, there is a brat. She'd make your Viscount Comey look positively sweet."

"I doubt that," Anna said, "though I'd wager my Pa could have given him a run for his money on being such a weasel."

"Why do you think he is here?" Lady Matilda asked.

"I'd wager he's out of money again. It seems to slip through his fingers like sand," Lady Tremaine said sadly. "He's nothing like his departed father—my brother. He was almost miserly, he kept such a tight hold on the estate finances. William's allowance is not as large as perhaps a man of his station should be because of that—but my brother did not trust him not to waste his inheritance before he reached his majority."

"And that will be soon?" Anna asked curiously.

"Not for another eight years. William will not come of age until he is thirty-five. If he wishes to get his hands on his funds earlier, he must marry. I can only assume that is why he is so ever-present, in London and now here in Bath. He must hope to find himself a young and foolish heiress to give him control of his estate."

This made sense to Anna. It must be frustrating to know that you have everything you need and not be able to access it. She'd known the misery of never having anything, but it would have been much harder to bear if there had ever been, just out of reach, the means with which to change everything. Viscount Comey must chomp at the bit for the day when he would come into his own. His impatience and rudeness seemed a little more understandable—even if she still thought him to be the most odious of creatures.

"Then perhaps we should find him one, so he might then leave us alone," Lady Matilda said firmly.

"I'd not wish my great-nephew on any decent young lady," Lady Tremaine said darkly. "He'd make of her life a living hell."

"Then we find him one that isn't any better than he is," Lady Matilda said simply. "He has a title and will inherit yours in time and has a considerable inheritance and one to come—he is, whether we like it or not, a catch in this dreadful world of ours. How hard can it be to find someone as venal as he is to fit his needs?"

Anna nodded her agreement. "If I am right and his curiosity about Amelia Hartley is due to her wealth, then it would seem that his only criteria for a match must be that they have wealth they can bring to the union." Lady Jane would have done just that, and as far as Anna could see it would be the only thing that her sweet friend and the heiress to a sugar trading company might have in common.

The at home was busy when they arrived at Mr. Hartley's fine townhouse later that afternoon. Mrs. Hartley welcomed them in and seemed delighted to meet Viscount Comey. He, in turn, was delighted to find that Miss Amelia Hartley had come to stay with her aunt and uncle for the next month. Mr. Hartley called her over and introduced them all. Miss Hartley was effusive in her greeting of Lady Matilda and Lady Tremaine, fawned over Viscount Comey, and barely even noticed Anna long enough to say good day.

In no time at all, Viscount Comey had lured Miss Hartley away towards the pianoforte, where he played adequately enough, and they sang duets together in slightly off-key voices. Anna was delighted when Mr. Hartley stepped forward and insisted that Lady Matilda play for the gathered company for a time. Amelia had pouted; she took his interference as an insult, but she had not gainsaid her uncle. She stood up and curtseyed to Lady Matilda, who graciously smiled at her as Viscount Comey offered Miss Hartley his arm and escorted her to the punchbowl where he poured her a glass. They sat in a nearby window seat, and though they were both silent for a moment, it was not long before they had struck up a stilted conversation.

Amelia was not a happy young woman, from all Anna could glean from watching her interact with Viscount Comey and the other people present. She possessed a fine allowance and was heir to a very profitable trading company, but she was a plain girl with a dumpy figure and a sharp tongue that must have made her unpopular when she attended her only Season two years earlier. Anna couldn't help thinking that perhaps the pair deserved one another. Miss Hartley was seeking betterment and anyone without a title simply was not worth her wasting time upon, which was why she'd not been even polite when greeting Anna, who was only a lady's companion.

It was a relief when Lady Tremaine announced that she wished to return home to rest. Anna helped her into the carriage and then followed her inside and sat opposite her. Lady Matilda wished to stay a little longer, so she had asked if they could send the carriage back for her later. Viscount Comey showed no desire to leave, and Anna was relieved that she and Lady Tremaine would be traveling alone. It was hard to remain polite to someone she felt was up to no good.

Back at the house, Anna read in the library whilst Lady Tremaine napped. She heard the click of the front door as Viscount Comey returned. She turned her attention back to her book, sure that he would not disturb her. But instead of him heading up the stairs to his rooms, she heard the clatter of his boots crossing the marble floor towards the library doors. He flung them wide and marched into the room. He stood for a moment, then turned and slammed the doors behind him. Anna realized that he hadn't yet seen her and was not aware of her presence. She didn't know whether to stand up and announce herself or to wait quietly until he addressed her.

He looked around the room, and finally, his eyes alighted upon her. "Miss Campbell, what a surprise," he said, his tone unusually polite. "I hope you had a lovely afternoon." Anna felt her hackles rise. There was nothing outwardly threatening here, yet she sensed danger in every part of her being. Viscount Comey rarely so much as glanced at her, much less struck up a conversation with her.

"I did, thank you, my Lord," she said, standing up politely as she had been taught to do. "Did you enjoy meeting Miss Hartley?" She wondered if he would think her rude if she made her excuses to leave. There was still so much about this new life that she did not understand – that one must be polite even to those one despised, and to accept men's interest even if it made one's skin crawl.

"I did," Viscount Comey said, his smile thin and did not quite reach his eyes, which were dark and almost sinister-looking "But I must confess to you, Miss Campbell, she is not as intriguing to me as you are." He moved closer, his voice soft and his smile as warm as he was able to muster, which merely made him seem even more weasel-like and unpleasant than usual.

Anna wished she could take a step back, but to do so would seem dreadfully rude. She felt as though he were backing her into a corner, and she did not know why. She needed to think quickly, so she might keep him at arm's length until she had worked out why he was being so oddly charming. "I am not intriguing, my Lord," she said. "I am no more than I seem."

"Come, Miss Campbell. I think we both know that is not the case," Viscount Comey said, still smiling. His eyes sparkled with something, not mischief exactly, but it was as if he were a cat toying with a mouse that he knew he'd be able to catch and devour when he was ready. "I think we both know that you have ulterior motives for being here, in my great-aunt's household."

"I do not know what you mean," Anna said firmly. Viscount Comey was now no more than a few feet away from her. She could smell the scent of his sweat, his horse's sweat, and the pomade he used upon his hair. Anna's skin prickled, and she had to resist the urge to wrinkle up her nose in disgust at his pungent proximity.

"Come now; you don't need to lie to me. After all, we're both here for the same thing, aren't we?" he reached out and took one of her curls between his finger and thumb. He twirled it absent-mindedly around them before he tucked it behind her ear. It was an unexpected and unwanted intimate gesture. Anna flinched, unable to stop her instinctive reaction to resist this man and get away from him. If she was still Pa's daughter, and not Lady Tremaine's companion she would have given him a sharp knee to his breeches and been long gone from here by now – but she did not think such behavior would be forgiven, even by the kindly Lady Tremaine.

"Come now; no need to be so shy," he said, his voice low and seductive, or it would have been if he weren't so repellent to her. "I want her money; you want her money. We'd do well to make a pact so we both get what we want."

Anna took a step backward. Viscount Comey continued to move closer, and Anna kept moving away until her back was against the wall. He slipped his hand around her waist, letting it rest in the small of Anna's back. "I'd advise you to step away, my Lord," Anna said. She did not want to let Lady Tremaine down, did not wish to be unladylike, but the street urchin inside of her was nearing the surface with every passing moment.

"Why, I could be helpful to you, and you could be helpful to me," he wheedled, then pressed his lips to hers. Anna tried to push him away, but he was stronger than his slender frame belied. He pushed closer and tried to force open her lips with his tongue.

She was about to raise her knee to kick him between

his legs, as Pa had always taught her to do, her desire to be the good young lady that Lady Tremaine wished her to be worn too thin, when the door of the library opened, and Lady Tremaine entered. Her expression showed her deep dismay and shock at finding Anna and Viscount Comey pressed up against the wall in what must have seemed to be a passionate embrace.

"What in tarnation is going on here?" she demanded.

"I...I...I didn't want it," Anna stuttered.

Viscount Comey stepped away, wiped his lips, and smirked. "I always said she was just after your money," he said smugly. "Why, she threw herself at me, like the common hussy she is. You should never have trusted her."

"Your Ladyship, you know I would never do such a thing," Anna pleaded. "You know how I feel about him – and about you. I would never do such a thing."

"I know I said you might make a match," Lady Tremaine said, her kindly face no longer looking at either of them with warmth and affection. She was angrier than Anna could ever have imagined her being. "I did not mean you to do so by such underhand means. Mayhaps William was right about you all along. If you could lie to me about your feelings for him, then do this behind my back, I am not sure that I can trust you."

"But he is lying," Anna protested, tears pricking at her eyes as she realized how unfair everything was for women like her, and always would be. She'd not ever thought that Lady Tremaine would take Viscount Comey's side over hers, not if she had been given a chance to explain what had really happened. But it seemed that when push came to shove, her Pa had been right. The aristocracy would always look after their own.

"Get out of my house," Lady Tremaine ordered Anna. "I'll not have a liar in my household. I expected your loyalty, after everything I have done for you, that this is the manner in which you repay me is not something I ever expected of you. I should have always remembered where you came from. I never want to see you again."

Anna felt bitter tears of anger, of betrayal, and of shame begin to pour down her cheeks. She looked from Lady Tremaine to Viscount Comey and realized that she would never be able to explain what had happened. Despite everything, despite how close she believed she and Lady Tremaine had become, Anna would always be the common peasant that had been picked up by the roadside. Viscount Comey had gotten his way. He'd been just as cunning as she had suspected he was—and now she would be banished forever.

CHAPTER THIRTEEN

"My Lord, they told me nobody lived there of that name," the boy said, his voice quavering a little as if he expected to be scolded for not having delivered Edward's letter to Miss Campbell. "I tried to get them to check, but they was very certain."

His words made Edward more anxious than he could possibly say. He knew full well that Miss Campbell had left for Bath with Lady Tremaine and that they would be staying with Viscount Kingston. If the servants there had told this lad that there was nobody there of that name, Edward could only assume that she had been let go for some reason. He could not think of a single thing that would have made his godmother part with her beloved companion. Lady Frances loved Miss Campbell. She'd even spoken to her lawyers about having her written into her will. So, the news he was receiving made no sense to him.

He dismissed the boy and tucked the letter back into his jacket pocket. If he could, he'd ride to Bath forthwith—but he had business to attend to that simply could not wait, here in London. He tried to rationalize that he'd know soon enough what was happening. Mama was traveling to Bath today; she would find out the truth of the matter. But he couldn't stop a shudder passing through his body, and he acknowledged his fear. He wished that his message could have reached Miss Campbell, and he feared what might have happened in the meantime to her—and to Lady Frances. Viscount Comey was trouble for them both, and Edward dreaded learning of what might happen next.

Having told his mother what he had learned, Edward went to Parliament, where he sat through hours of inter-minably dull rhetoric and wished that he had followed his instincts and dropped everything to go to Bath—but he had made a promise to Prinny that he would help him and his faction in Parliament to pass this bill. He could not renege upon a promise to the Regent, or to his friend, and so, dutifully, he remained in town and prayed every minute as he sat on the benches of the chamber that Miss Campbell might come to him for help if she needed it.

He did not return to his home until late that night. A platter of cold cuts had been laid out for him for his supper, along with a decanter of claret. Edward took it into the library and sat down in front of the fire to eat. He poured a large measure of the rich red wine and drank deeply. He could not reconcile himself to the fact that even though he had tried to warn Miss Campbell, he had ultimately failed in his endeavor. He wondered where she would have gone. He doubted if she would have returned to London, though he recalled her speaking of an aunt that she thought might live there.

He sat up. Of course. Miss Campbell had an aunt. He might not have been able to prevent her from falling into whatever trap Comey had set for her, but Edward could locate her relatives—and her. He'd put his lawyers onto it first thing. He did not doubt that they would know somebody with the skills necessary to find people—no matter how well they may try to hide. Feeling a little more reassured that there was still something he might do to be able to help Miss Campbell, he set about eating his supper with gusto.

He dozed by the fire after he'd finished his repast, waking when the clock on the mantel struck midnight. He got up wearily and made his way out of the library and across the hallway to the stairs. He'd barely made it up three steps when there was a loud knocking on the door. Edward almost jumped out of his skin at the noise. Nobody came to call at this hour—unless something dreadful had occurred.

Rather than waiting for one of the servants to appear so they might open the door, Edward jumped down from the stairs and then half-ran across the hallway. He opened the door and heaved a huge sigh of relief. "Thank heaven you are safe," he said as he pulled Miss Campbell into his arms and held her tightly to his body. She dropped her bag and put her arms around his waist, tears pouring down her cheeks, soaking his shirt. She was cold as ice, despite the mildness of the early summer evening. "Come inside. You must get warm and tell me everything."

Phinney, his valet, appeared just as Edward shut the door behind Miss Campbell, Annie, the parlor maid and Mrs. Chilton, the housekeeper, just behind him. They looked at Edward with wide eyes. "Miss Campbell is to stay with us for a few days," he said in a tone that would brook no refusal. "Have the pink rooms made ready; bring us some hot chocolate and something to eat into the library."

They nodded and disappeared, but Edward could hear them muttering amongst themselves as they departed. He did not care what they thought, though. All he cared about was making sure that Miss Campbell was alright—and that his godmother was not in any danger. He ushered Miss Campbell into the warmth of the library, letting his hand rest in the small of her back. She was clearly exhausted, her face was pale, and she was shivering like a leaf.

"I am sorry," she said once he'd sat her down. He knelt before her and took her hands in his, rubbing them gently to warm them. "I should not have come, but I did not know who else to turn to."

"Miss Campbell, tell me what happened?" Edward said as Annie appeared with hot chocolate and a warm blanket. Edward tucked it around Miss Campbell's legs and let her take a few sips of the sweet and warming beverage. "Annie, will you stay with us?" he asked the maid, cautious of ensuring that Miss Campbell's virtue would not be compromised by their being alone. Annie nodded, and took a seat in the furthest corner of the room, out of earshot, but where she could see everything.

"I don't rightly know what happened," Miss Campbell said sadly. "I knew Viscount Comey was up to something, but I did not know what. It all happened so suddenly."

"What happened so suddenly?" Edward asked, moving from the floor before her to sit in the chair by her side.

"Everything was going well," Miss Campbell said, her beautiful face streaked with grime from her travels and the tears she'd just shed. Edward had never seen her look more lovely or more tragic. "Lady Tremaine was much improved; she was quite her old self again. She took the waters every day, and she rested, and I was so happy to see her as she was."

"Then what happened?" Edward prompted her.

"Then Viscount Comey arrived—unannounced as ever. He was clearly angry that his betrothal to Lady Jane Fairley had come to an end. I think he blamed me. Yet he seemed unusually polite to me—it set my teeth on edge because it was so unusual."

Edward nodded and watched as she took another sip of the chocolate. She seemed so much quieter, somehow smaller than she had been before. Whatever had happened, it had changed her, made her doubt herself in every way. Edward wanted someone to blame for it. He hated to see her so unhappy.

"Viscount Comey seemed to be interested in the daughter of some merchant," Miss Campbell continued. "They were very cozy when we went to visit with her aunt and uncle a few days ago. But then he came home that night, and he was trying to seduce me—I think." She blanched as she said this; even the memory of what had happened was enough to make her feel fear, and there was a flash of rage in her eyes, too, as she began to quake again. "He pushed me up against the wall and tried to kiss me."

"I see," Edward said tightly, trying to crush down the feelings of jealousy and rage that threatened to over-take him. He wanted to kill Comey for such behavior. Miss Campbell was not in a position to demand that Viscount Comey not force himself upon her. As Lady Tremaine's companion, she was merely a servant; she could not have told him no. If she did, she would have risked her place in the household—and it seemed that even though she had acquiesced, she had lost all anyway.

"Lady Tremaine came in, and she saw us. Without even waiting to ask me what was happening, she banished me from the house. She was not herself. She seemed quite irrational, and though she may be eccentric, she is never that. It was as if something had come over her. She would never normally have not given me a chance to explain." Miss Campbell's voice was now flat. The rage she felt towards Comey was not echoed in the feelings she felt to her employer—but Edward wasn't entirely sure what she felt towards Lady Frances at all. He would have understood if Miss Campbell felt in some way betrayed or let down, but her flat tone and blank eyes gave him no clues.

"Miss Campbell, I'm so sorry. I don't know what to say, and I know that sorry isn't enough—but I wish this hadn't happened to you. I shall write to my godmother immediately, and will tell her your side of things. I am sure she would reconsider if she knew what had really happened."

"That is kind of you, though I doubt it would do much good," Miss Campbell said, her tone filled with her sense of defeat. "But you need not apologize. It was not you that did those things. I blame nobody but him for his actions. But I fear for Lady Tremaine."

"She banished you for something he did, and you are still concerned for her welfare?" Edward said, utterly shocked by her revelation. In her shoes, he would have been livid. Would have wanted revenge upon them both. But Miss Campbell was, again, showing the innate decency she possessed; her kindness and concern for others was just one of the many reasons that he had come to love her.

"I am. I think he did what he did on purpose. I would not be surprised to learn that he perhaps asked his great-aunt to seek him out in the library, knowing he would be able to create such a tableau as he did, just for her. He kept insisting that I was after the same thing that he was —Lady Tremaine's fortune. I have never sought her money and insisted that I pay her back for every gown, every entertainment from my wages. I refused to take them, even when I left, though the Kingston's house-keeper and cook both urged me to do so. I could not have her thinking I was only after her money."

"I know you were not, and when things settle, I am sure that she will know you weren't, too," Edward assured her. "My godmother can be a little rash, and makes decisions and judgments too rapidly at times. Sometimes that proves to be to her benefit – as it did when she decided to take you in from the roadside, though others are less wise. I know that whenever Comey is around, she is on edge. He makes her behave very differently, you must have noticed that?"

"He rattles us all," Miss Campbell agreed. She paused for a moment, her gentle eyes searching his face. "You did not seem surprised when I said I feared she might be in danger."

"No, I am not," Edward said with a sigh. He reached for his jacket that he'd left over the back of the sofa on which Miss Campbell was now sitting. He pulled out the note he'd tried to get to Miss Campbell from his pocket. "I tried to send you this." He handed it to her.

She set her chocolate down upon the table to her left and broke the seal upon the paper. She unfolded it and read the letter he'd sent. She bit at her lip as the words sank in. "You fear she is in danger, too—and that I was. Well, Comey has managed to remove me from the picture, but Lady Tremaine was hale and hearty that day, though I was not so sure of that when I left."

"My mother has set out for Bath today, and Lady Tremaine will likely move from Viscount Kingston's home to theirs when she arrives. I don't think even Comey would dare to do anything to Lady Frances whilst she is under my parents' roof and my mother's hawk-like eye, so I do not think we need fear for her for the rest of the summer."

"You are sure of that?" Miss Campbell said, her eyes beseeching him for his reassurance. Edward wasn't certain, but he did know that his mother would not let

Comey in her house, so Lady Frances would be as safe as anyone could make her.

"I won't ever lie to you, Miss Campbell. I cannot be utterly sure of it, but I know Mama is already on her guard and will be wary of Comey. Lady Frances is as safe as she can be."

"Thank you," Miss Campbell said as she made to get up. "I should go now. I just could not wait to let you know. I knew you would do what you could to protect Lady Tremaine. I have taken up enough of your time. Thank you, Lord Westerham."

She was already half-way to the door before Edward realized that she meant to leave. "No, Miss Campbell, you must stay," he said, hurrying after her. "It is late, the streets are dangerous, and you yourself said that you have nowhere to go. Given everything you have done for me, and for my godmother—though she may not realize it—I cannot let you go without doing something to help you."

"I don't need anything," Miss Campbell said. "Though I thank you for your kindness."

"Nonsense. You need a family, a place to stay—or a position," Edward insisted. "And I shall help you find one, or all of them. Now, there is a room upstairs with a big, comfortable bed. I shall have Annie bring you up a bath in the morning and shall set my lawyers to finding your aunt first thing. Until we find her, you must stay here."

"That is too kind of you."

"And don't worry about your reputation," Edward insisted. "I will arrange for a companion first thing, so that is all is proper in this house. Perhaps Mary Cordwainer might join you for a time until we can arrange something more permanent?"

"Thank you," Miss Campbell said, with a tear in her eye, knowing she had nowhere else to go.

Edward was as good as his word. He sent for Miss Campbell's dear friend, who came at once, while he arranged interviews to appoint a more suitable permanent companion. He wrote to his godmother on Miss Campbell's behalf and had indeed gone to his lawyers and set them on the path to finding Miss Campbell's long-lost family, but the search for them was not as simple a task as he'd originally anticipated.

Days turned into weeks and weeks into months as they waited for news. Nothing seemed forthcoming from either source. Miss Campbell fretted every day that she was too much trouble, that having a young woman in his house could only be damaging to his reputation—though not once did she ever seem to be concerned about her own. He assured her that there was no impropriety, that the presence of the wonderful Mrs Hatton protected them both, but still she worried.

As time had passed, Edward had become used to her presence. He found himself listening for the sound of her footsteps upon the stair each morning. He delighted in the way she smiled at him shyly as she entered the dining room as if she still did not believe that she belonged there. She brightened up his days, and though the *ton* had long since departed for their estates or to Bath for the summer, Edward had never loved London more. As September ticked over into October, Edward had come to think that their quiet way of being together was all he would ever want or need in life.

So, he wasn't sure if he was happy or sad when his lawyers finally sent word that they had located Miss Campbell's aunt and uncle. Mr. Albert Trimble and his wife, Mrs. Hannah Trimble, lived in Portsmouth. They were successful merchants, specializing in fine woolens and textiles. Mr. Trimble owned three ships outright, and they had two daughters and a son. They would be delighted for Miss Campbell to join them in their home.

He fingered the letter that they had sent for Miss Campbell and wondered if he could ever bear to part with her. She was more than just someone who shared his home. He had always known that—though she had never given him any inkling that she might feel anything more for him than friendship. The very idea of her moving to Portsmouth and him never seeing her again tore his heart into tiny pieces. But she deserved to know. She had suffered so much and been so very brave for far too long.

Taking large strides, he made his way to the front parlor, where he knew he would find her at this time of day because she always said that the light in that room was best for embroidery. He found her poring over a colorful design, with gorgons and dragons on it, that he'd challenged her to create as he so loved mythical creatures. She had created a veritable bestiary of peculiar creatures for him, and he knew that he would treasure it always.

"Miss Campbell," he said softly, not wanting to disturb her too greatly if she was undertaking a tricky stitch. She looked up and beamed at him. Edward felt his heart crack again as he wondered if she knew just how much of an impact her happiness had upon his. "I have some news."

He handed her the letter and watched her face as she read it. Tears began to flood down her cheeks, and she looked up at him with wide eyes. "You found them," she said softly. "And they want me."

He'd never felt so sad when he realized just how desperately she had longed for somewhere to belong. She'd thought she had found a home with Lady Frances, only for it to be snatched away from her—and she believed that he only wanted her until she found somewhere else. He wished that he could tell her just how he felt about her. He wished he could tell her that he would have given her a home, with him, with his love, from the very first. But he knew he could not, and so he kept quiet.

"You truly have been so kind, and I cannot thank you enough for this," she added, flinging her arms around his neck and kissing his cheek. He turned his head, without even thinking and the kiss landed upon his lips instead. His body reacted to the inadvertent touch immediately, sending a shiver of pleasure from top to toe. She looked surprised, but she did not pull away, and though he knew he should not, Edward let his arms twine around her waist and kissed her back.

CHAPTER FOURTEEN

Portsmouth was busy and loud. Anna's aunt and uncle lived not far from the dock, where their ships came and went out on their journeys to far-flung lands Anna couldn't even imagine. They'd once lived above the warehouse where Uncle Albert stored his goods, right on the dock itself. They had made her welcome right from the first. Her cousins did not seem at all jealous of her as she was dragged to every event her aunt could think of so she might be introduced to everyone they knew.

Yet despite their warmth and kindness, Anna missed Edward. She missed Lady Tremaine—and she simply could not stop worrying about what might happen to her old employer. She knew all too well that with the summer now long gone that Lady Tremaine would have returned to Trelawney Hall, and that there would be nobody there —except the staff—who might look out for her welfare. Edward had promised that he would visit regularly and had assured her that so would his mother—but Anna couldn't shake the feeling of foreboding that seemed to overshadow the happiness she should have been feeling in her new life.

She thought often about the kiss that Edward had given her the day he'd gotten the news about her aunt and uncle's whereabouts. She had never felt that way before, as if she was melting in someone's arms. His lips had been so soft and tender—not like the almost bruising kiss that Viscount Comey had inflicted upon her. It had been searching and sweet—though both of them had known, even as they embraced, that they could never take it further. Their parting had been bittersweet—both had their regrets, and both knew it was for the best, but it had been the hardest thing Anna had ever done.

He'd promised to write to her, but she'd heard nothing from him, and she did not dare write to him first. She tried each day to accept that it was over, that brilliant, and utterly surreal part of her life where she had moved amongst royalty and had the friendship of lords and ladies was done. Now, she was simply Anna once more, and though her life was infinitely more comfortable than it had ever been when she'd lived with her father, it did not resemble in any way the rarified heights that had temporarily been her home.

So, when she made her way home after church on the Sunday before Advent began, she was surprised to see a phaeton outside the house. Nobody she knew in Portsmouth could ever have afforded such an impractical vehicle—and she shuddered when she thought of the only other man she'd ever known to drive such a carriage.

But it was silly to think that Viscount Comey would be here, at her aunt's house. He'd probably not given her a second thought once he'd manipulated his great-aunt into seeing her off. But that thought didn't stop her from feeling apprehensive as she let herself in.

"Anna, your friend is here, from London," Mary, the maid, said as she took Anna's hat and gloves and set them on the hat stand, then waited as Anna took off her coat and handed it to her to hang up, too.

"My friend from London?" Anna queried.

"Yes, the handsome gentleman that brought you here," Mary said. "He seemed ever so solemn when he got here. I do hope that there is nothing wrong."

Anna felt her pulse quicken. "So do I, Mary," she said fervently. "So do I."

She hurried to the parlor. She could hear Lord Westerham's rich baritone before she even reached the door. She leaned against the wall and took a couple of deep, calming breaths before she opened the door and went inside. Lord Westerham jumped to his feet and moved to greet her. He took her arms in his hands and kissed both cheeks, much to Anna's surprise. "Dear Miss Campbell, I am so sorry to have come without warning, but I had to let you know—and after last time when my message did not get through, I trusted nobody but myself," he said, his eyes full of concern.

"Lord Westerham, tell me, whatever is the matter?" Anna said urgently.

"It is Lady Tremaine; she is sick. The doctor says that she is at death's door."

"Then we must go to her at once," Anna said, knowing that there was no other course of action that she could bear. If Lady Tremaine needed her, then she had to go.

"I thought you would say that. I have arranged for fresh horses along the journey. Do you need long to pack?"

"No, I need very little. Just give me fifteen minutes."

She'd barely even noticed her aunt, seated behind Lord Westerham, but she stood up now and put an arm around Anna's shoulders. "I shall help you, though I am sad that we shall lose you so soon after we finally found you."

"Thank you so very much, Aunt Hannah," Anna said, turning to hug her aunt gratefully. "I am sure I shall return soon, but I cannot leave her alone when she is sick. She was so good to me."

"And she threw you out," Uncle Albert reminded her.

"She did, but I think she was manipulated by the same man that is probably responsible for her being sick," Anna said, trying to explain, but knowing that her aunt and uncle would never understand. "Lady Tremaine gave me everything. Without her, I'd never have known Lord Westerham—and without him, I'd never have found you, my dear family."

She reached out and kissed her uncle on the cheek, touched that they were so concerned for her. Pa had never much noticed her—unless she was of use to him. Her relationship with Lady Tremaine was complicated, but that was not a reason to abandon her when her need was greatest. At last, Anna had a way to truly pay her back for everything she had been given. She would not rest until that debt was repaid.

Edward was an excellent driver, and Anna was astounded at how quickly they got to Trelawney Hall. As he'd told her, he'd arranged for fresh horses at every stage of their journey, and so they had traveled through the night to get to Lady Tremaine's side as soon as was possible. Edward had barely brought the phaeton to a stop before she leaped out of the carriage and raced up the steps, barged through the front doors, and raced up the stairs to Lady Tremaine's bedchamber.

She heard voices as she approached. "She is fading fast, my Lord," a voice she thought she knew, but couldn't quite place, was saying.

"She'll not last the night?" Viscount Comey's whine asked.

"I'd not be able to tell you, my Lord. She's tougher than most; she may still make a full recovery." The unknown man's voice was hopeful. Anna almost snorted with derision; Viscount Comey wouldn't want that one little bit, of that she was certain.

"It is what I wish for with all my heart," Viscount Comey said with the utmost insincerity.

The door opened, and Dr. Winston emerged. Seeing his face, Anna knew why his voice had been so familiar. He was the physician that had attended her almost exactly a year ago when she'd been run over by that carriage. He looked grave. Anna did not doubt that he would be doing all he could to make his patient well—but she wondered if he knew just what he might be up against, and what he should be looking for to do so.

Anna slipped into the chamber. Viscount Comey was stood beside the bed, looking at his great-aunt with the most peculiar expression upon his face. He looked delighted. Anna barged him away from the bed. "I don't know what you have done to her, but I will not let you get away with it," she said fiercely.

"You do not belong in this house," Viscount Comey said derisively. "You have no say here and never did—no matter how much my great-aunt may have let you get away with in the past. She saw through you—you manipulative little minx. You were only ever after her money. That you would dare to come back here after you disappointed her so... You broke her heart."

"As if you'd care one jot about that, Comey," Lord Westerham said as he strode into the room behind them. He stood by Anna and took her hand. She felt buoyed by his support. He made her stronger, braver—better. "I think you just described yourself when you spoke about only wanting the money. How much debt are you in now? Did you manage to find the payments for the last two quarters? I heard that Miss Hartley turned down your proposal, too. Things really weren't going your way, and so you decided to hasten your great-aunt's passing, did you?"

"What did you do, slip her a little bit of poison each day, just enough to make her sicker and sicker, but not enough to kill her outright?" Anna asked. She'd known women do such things to their abusive husbands, weakening them just enough that they would seem to have died of natural causes. "How did you do it when you weren't staying with us, when she got ill in London? Was it the valet I saw you with?"

Viscount Comey spluttered his indignation but seemed incapable of mustering an eloquent response. Anna gave him a look of utter disgust and turned away from him and sat down beside Lady Tremaine, on the very edge of the bed. She reached out her hand and placed it on the older woman's forehead. She was burning up. Anna took up a cloth from the basin beside the bed and dipped it into the water, wrung it out, and then laid it over Lady Tremaine's temples. "Would you escort Viscount Comey from Trelawney Hall," she said to Lord Westerham. "I don't know who the local magistrate is, but I think it might be wise to take Viscount Comey straight to him."

Edward grimaced but he took Viscount Comey by the arm and pushed him down the stairs and then into the phaeton, binding his hands tightly. He drove swiftly to the grand manor of Sir Bartholomew Grahame, just two miles away. He dragged Comey to the door and explained why he was there. Sir Grahame was quick to usher them inside. "Do you have proof?" he asked Edward.

"Does information about the state of his debts count?" he asked.

"In part. It certainly explains why a man would do such a thing—but I need more than that. I need the poison—or testimony from Lady Tremaine that he did it," Sir Grahame warned Edward. "I can make sure he is kept under house arrest. But you know that there will be hell to pay if I cannot defend why I am doing such a thing to a peer of the realm."

"I'll get you the proof. Give me a fortnight. You shall have everything you need," Edward promised, shooting a look of pure hatred towards Comey, who just smirked.

"You'll never find a thing," he said arrogantly.

"I'd be quiet, my Lord," Sir Grahame told him. "You say things like that in my hearing, it just makes me think there is something to find." He turned back to Edward. "I'll send you a couple of my men; they'll know what they're looking for. Lady Tremaine has been a good friend to me. If there is any foul play here, I'll not let this toe-rag get away with it."

Feeling sure that he'd left Viscount Comey in the right place, Edward made his way back to Trelawney Hall, where he began to search high and low for the evidence that Sir Grahame had requested. Miss Campbell did not leave Lady Tremaine's side, not even to sleep or eat. Selflessly, she took care of his godmother day in and day out. They were both rewarded on a day when snow had fallen outside the Hall, frosting the grounds, so they resembled a winter wonderland. Edward was rummaging in one of the attics, just above Viscount Comey's suite of rooms, when he heard Miss Campbell's voice calling out for him.

"Lord Westerham, come quickly," she cried.

Edward dropped the box he was holding and turned to hurry down the stairs. The box landed on the floor, and a couple of the items inside rolled out and then disappeared into the darkness. Edward knelt to reach for them, only to find not only were they not there but that there was a hidden hole in the floorboards. He inched closer, so he could reach his arm inside and feel around more easily. He pulled out old balls and books, but the thing that was most intriguing was a half-empty bottle of arsenic. It was clearly quite new, hadn't been put up there and forgotten, and Edward was sure that he had finally found what he was looking for.

Getting up, he hurried down to Lady Frances' rooms to find his godmother sitting up a little in bed, holding Miss Campbell's hand and smiling at her warmly. "I want the hall decorated immediately—and I will be well enough to host the ball," Lady Frances was saying firmly. "There has been a Christmas Eve Ball in this house for as long as it has existed. I will not be the first in my family to break with tradition."

Miss Campbell gave her an exasperated look. "I know better than to argue with you, but you need to rest, and Christmas Eve is only days away."

Edward chuckled. If his godmother was well enough to argue, then she was more than well enough to hold her annual ball. "Oh, I am so very glad to see you looking so much better," he said, moving to kiss her on the cheek. "Don't worry, Miss Campbell; I've found what I needed, so I am at your beck and call to get the house decorated perfectly for Christmas."

Miss Campbell gave him a withering glance, but then couldn't stop herself from grinning. "The pair of you are incorrigible," she said with a shrug. "I give in. I will speak with Cook, and we shall have the finest ball this house has ever seen." She got up and left the room, leaving Edward and his godmother alone.

"You brought my girl back to me," Lady Tremaine said, looking after Miss Campbell with fond but sad eyes. "She told me what truly happened that night. I don't know why I did not give her a chance to speak."

"I sent you a letter, soon after. Did you not receive it?"

Lady Frances shook her head. "I'd not heard from you, or your mother in some time. Now I think on it, I received very little mail from anyone at that time. I can only assume that William kept them from me somehow."

"I would not be surprised to find that to be true," Edward agreed.

"I know Willian can be sly as a fox – but I was so tired and so fraught with him being there. I reacted. I heard the rumors about her each time we went out—so much worse than when we had been in London. Everyone seemed to think that I shouldn't trust a girl with her upbringing. I don't deserve her kindness after what I did, but she came anyway."

"She is the very finest woman I know," Edward said truthfully. "I knew she would never forgive me if I didn't let her know you were sick."

"It was William, wasn't it?" Lady Tremaine confirmed. "He forced her, having spread rumors amongst Society in Bath, and amongst the Kingston's servants, that she was trying to get him to marry her—knowing that, of course, they would get back to me."

Edward nodded. "I certainly believe so," he said.

"She never wanted him to touch her that way. You know how much she disliked him. She never made a secret of it."

"Some girls would pretend not to like someone just so nobody notices that they do," Lady Tremaine said sagely. "But you are right, I should have known that she was never that kind of girl."

"I must go and tell my mother; she and Papa will be here any minute," Edward said. "She has been stopping by every day, too, since we learned of your ill health. She's been staying somewhere nearby—though she won't tell me where. She's been dreadfully mysterious."

Lady Tremaine giggled. "She's probably been staying at her brother's house," she said. "She'll never forgive me for telling you, but I am tired of all the lies and half-truths in my world."

"Her brother's house?" Edward asked.

"Indeed, the house she grew up in."

"But I thought she had no family, that they all passed away?"

"Not at all. They still live where they have always been. Your mother has just been embarrassed about them. You see, they lived in the lodge at the end of the driveway. Your mother's family have always been our gamekeepers."

Edward looked at her open-mouthed. Suddenly, there were a lot of things that seemed to slip into place. His mother's many disappearances whenever they came to visit Lady Frances, the way she often frowned when Papa or Lady Frances mentioned anything about their childhood. "Well, I never expected that," he said with a grin, knowing that, unwittingly, Lady Tremaine had just given him everything he needed to convince his parents to let him marry Miss Campbell. He leaned down and kissed her again, then went downstairs to wait for them to arrive.

EPILOGUE

Somehow, despite everything, Trelawney Hall was ready to host the biggest Christmas Eve Ball that had been held. After finding out about Lord Westerham's hidden family, Anna had asked Lady Tremaine to invite not just the *ton* but the staff and their families, and many of the villagers, too. Her aunt, uncle, and cousins would be arriving at any moment—and Anna had picked out some of the loveliest rooms in the house for them to stay in to celebrate Christmas with her, here. They would be going home on Twelfth Night.

She could hardly believe, as she got dressed up in a red silk gown, how much her life had changed in such a short period of time. This time last year, she had been hobbling around with a broken leg and a broken life. She'd watched as the lords and ladies, attending this event, had danced and had so much fun. She'd hardly believed that such pleasure was possible, and now she was getting ready to attend it herself.

She pinned her hair into place and made her way

downstairs. The ballroom was already beginning to fill up. She'd asked all of the women invited from Lady Tremaine's social set to bring an old gown that they no longer wore, the men any old jackets and breeches, and it had been delightful to watch the villagers and the staff get dressed up in their finery. They were stood now, looking a little anxious as they awaited the more fashionably late arrivals of *the Ton*.

Having an idea, Anna turned and went back upstairs, turning onto the Minstrel's gallery, where the musicians were playing some sedate tunes. "Do you know anything a little livelier?" she asked them.

"Of course, but Lady Tremaine usually wants us to be quiet and circumspect as the guests arrive," the violinist said.

"Don't worry about that," Anna assured him. "Tonight is not a normal night. Play something fun and loud. I want this party to start as it means to go on."

They all grinned at her and took up their instruments once more. They launched into a couple of sea shanties, which Anna could see were already having the desired effect as she hurried back to the dance floor. People had begun to dance and were whirling their partners around with gay abandon. Anna found herself whisked into the arms of one of the stable-hands, who grinned at her as they bounded around the floor. She laughed with absolute delight, threw her head back, and let herself dance as if nobody was watching.

❧

EDWARD ARRIVED with his parents not long after eight o'clock, but by the sound of the music and the shrieks and whoops coming from inside, the ball was already in full swing. He kissed his mother's cheek once they had handed over their coats to the maid, shook his father's hand, and then went in search of Miss Campbell. He entered the ballroom and stopped in his tracks. He couldn't help but see her in her vibrant red gown, her head tilted back, a smile of pure joy on her face. He smiled to see her so very happy, given everything that had happened to her over the past twelve months.

Lady Frances sidled up next to him and tucked her arm through his. "I have adopted her formally, you know," she said quietly. "And spoke with my lawyers and Prinny about changing the entail in her favor. She'll inherit everything I have, now that William is likely to spend the rest of his miserable life in jail. I'll still have to compensate him, but it seems a small price to pay."

"She won't want it," Edward replied.

"I know. She's told me that a hundred times. But it doesn't change it. She is the daughter I always longed for."

"Why did Mama keep her secret so long? Did she really think I'd ever think any less of her if I knew?"

"Your mother got so good at being what she wasn't that I think she'd convinced herself she'd never been anything else. I must confess, I think I tried to get Anna to do the same—but as you can see, thankfully, I haven't managed to do so."

"No, I don't think anyone could," Edward said, bending down to kiss the top of Lady France's head.

"Now, if you will excuse me, I have something very special I need to do."

Lady Frances clapped her hands delightedly. "The very best of luck, my boy," she said as he moved towards Miss Campbell and claimed her hand.

"This is a wonderful party," he told her as they galloped energetically across the floor. "I understand now what you meant when you said that you danced a little differently from what was on show last Christmas."

She laughed. "You remember that?"

"I do," he admitted. "I remember everything you've ever said to me."

"You do?" she asked, gasping for breath.

"Yes," he said, then grimaced as she was swept away from him by someone else.

Edward hurried after her and claimed her back. "Could we go somewhere a little quieter and talk?" he asked.

She nodded. "I am gasping for a drink. Every time I get close to the punch bowl, someone else grabs me, and whirls me away."

Edward took her hand and led her out of the ballroom, onto the terrace. He'd arranged with the stable-hands to light a path down towards the house his mother had grown up in, and Miss Campbell's eyes widened as she saw the blinking candles extending out across the grounds. He picked up a shawl he'd asked Lady Frances to leave on the terrace for just this moment and wrapped it around her shoulders. "Shall we?" he asked her.

She nodded, suddenly tongue-tied, and took his arm as they walked along the lighted path. When they reached the tiny gamekeeper's lodge, Lord Westerham stopped and took her hands in his.

"Dear Miss Campbell, we have both learned much about who we are and where we come from in these past twelve months. I like to think that I am a wiser man than the one that met you at the Christmas Eve Ball last year, but I am probably not. When we stopped the coach and took you in, I don't think any of us knew how our lives would change, but they have, and for the better in every way."

"How can you say that? Lady Tremaine was almost killed," Anna said, a little overwhelmed by everything that was happening on this most magical night.

"Besides that," Lord Westerham said. "Anna, I have brought you here because this is where my mother was born and raised."

Anna felt her mouth drop open. She would never have thought that the elegant countess could have been raised in such a humble setting. "Your mother lived here?" she asked, needing to be sure that she had heard him rightly.

"Indeed, she is a gamekeeper's daughter," Lord Westerham said with a chuckle. "It isn't important, but it hopefully will go some way towards making you say yes to what I have longed to ask you ever since last Christmas Eve."

"And what is that?" Anna asked, her stomach suddenly began to churn, and she felt her skin get hot and clammy as Lord Westerham took her hands in his and gazed into her eyes.

"Will you marry me, Anna Campbell? Will you be my wife?"

"Are you quite mad?" she asked him, her eyes wide with surprise. "I am the daughter of a card sharper, a thief, a man who sold half-broken horses and left town before the buyers realized they'd got a killer on their hands. I'm not fit for marriage to a man like you."

Lord Westerham simply waved his hand at the tiny house behind them. "I've already established that my bloodline is not so perfect, either," he said with a grin. "And, you aren't simply Anna Campbell anymore, are you?"

Anna flushed. She still thought it peculiar that she should be addressed now as Lady Anna Tremaine. "I suppose I am not," she admitted.

"So, will you stop making excuses and tell me whether you will make me the happiest man alive?" Lord Westerham begged her. "I love you, Lady Anna Campbell Tremaine. You have held my heart for months now. I'd like you to hold it forever."

"Oh, yes," she sighed as he took her in his arms and kissed her tenderly. "You see, I have loved you from the very first, too. Oh, this truly is the most magical Christmas. Now I will truly be part of a family."

"Shall we go inside and tell everyone our good news, dearest Anna?"

"I think we should, darling Edward, but only after you kiss me again, so I know that all of this is real."

I HOPE you enjoyed Anna and Edward's story!

If you are in the mood for Christmas stories, I have two other books available. Mistletoe Magic...turn a few pages for a sneak peak!

And Love and Christmas Wishes: Three Regency Romance Novellas

A SNEAK PEEK OF MISTLETOE MAGIC

PROLOGUE

"Georgiana?"

Georgiana, who had been busying herself with her needlework on what was otherwise a very damp and cold winter's day, lifted her head as her brother walked into the drawing-room.

"Ah, Georgiana, there you are," he said, a kind smile on his face and a sharp look in his eyes that sent a twinge of concern into Georgiana's heart. "Might I pry you away from your needlework for a moment?"

Georgiana looked at her brother steadily, taking him in. The Earl had become much more amenable of late, given he had married a little less than a year ago, but with the look in his eye at present, Georgiana felt herself become somewhat unsettled. Something was afoot, and she was not sure she would like whatever it was.

"Georgiana?"

She blinked. "Oh, yes," she said, realizing she had not yet answered the question. "Yes, of course, Allerton."

Setting her needlework on the arm of the chair, she looked up at him expectantly.

"Good." He beamed at her as though he were certain she would be pleased with whatever it was he had to offer her. "You are aware, I hope, of the little Season that is due to start very soon?"

Georgiana frowned. The summer Season had been her third foray into society, for she had made her come out some two years ago but had then been invited to Bath for her second Season by a very close friend of her late mother, Lady Clarence. Her brother had been more than pleased for her to go; it had meant he would have less responsibility and, therefore, more freedom to do as he wished. She had spent the winter with Lord and Lady Clarence, enjoying the little Season, only to hear a very strange rumor being thrown around Bath that the Earl of Allerton was to marry—and to marry soon. What a shock it had been to hear that this rumor was, in fact, nothing short of the truth! At first, she had thought him to be making a mockery of her and thus had not wanted to believe it, but by the time the wedding came around, Georgiana had very little idea *but* to accept that her brother was to marry! Thankfully, his choice of bride had been most excellent indeed, and since that time, Georgiana had found Lady Alice Allerton to be kindness itself. This home had been happier than ever before, and their lives on the estate brought them all some quiet contentment.

It now seemed that this contentedness was to be shattered.

"I have it in my mind to take us all to London!" her

brother exclaimed, throwing up his hands as if excited himself at the prospect. "I know that your summer Season went very well indeed, but since no offers of marriage came to you, I think it best that we return to London for the winter Season also."

Georgiana looked up into her brother's face and felt her stomach tighten. Yes, the summer Season had gone well, but her brother was correct to say she had received no proposals. The gentlemen had been charming enough, and one or two had called on her a good many times, but none had sought to take matters any further. Georgiana had not known why. Was it because she was on her third Season and therefore considered to be almost on the shelf? Or was it because they believed her brother would give her no great dowry, given he had married Alice for her wealth?

"What say you, Georgiana?" her brother asked, beaming at her as though she ought to be practically dancing around the room in joy. "We shall once again go to London, and you shall have another opportunity to find a suitable match."

Georgiana bit her lip. "Brother, whilst I am truly grateful to you for your willingness to aid me in this matter, I fear it will be of no use."

Lord Allerton's face darkened, the smile fading away and his eyes losing some of their brightness. "What can you mean?"

"Well," Georgiana said, speaking in very practical terms. "I have been in London for two summer Seasons and in Bath for one, but as yet, I have not found a single gentleman to seek my hand in marriage. I fear," she continued, forcing her own emotions down so she could speak without her voice shaking or her eyes filling with tears. "I fear it might be quite impossible for me to do so even during the little Season, Allerton. I am perhaps now considered to be 'on the shelf,' or mayhap there is a worry that my dowry might be a good deal smaller than what a gentleman would expect." She dropped her eyes from her brother's face, seeing his sharp look and not wanting him to feel any guilt over what she was saying. "I fear that another Season will not bring about what you expect."

There was silence for some time. Georgiana did not know where to look, her heart aching as she let her gaze drift around the room. When she finally dared a glance at her brother, she saw that his brows were low over his eyes and that his expression was shuttered. She could not tell what he was feeling, praying he did not think she was attempting to blame him in any way for her present unmarried state. Dropping her head, Georgiana pressed her lips together tightly, wondering if she should say anything more.

"I have it!"

Her breath caught as she shot a look up to her brother who was, much to her astonishment, now grinning from ear to ear.

"Allerton?" she queried slowly, butterflies beginning to beat their wings furiously in the pit of her stomach. "What is it?"

"I have it," he said again, coming towards her and crouching down so he might look up into her face. His hand found hers, and he squeezed her fingers tightly. "You have every right to worry," he continued as she swallowed hard. "It is not because you are not lovely in every way that the gentlemen do not wish to draw near to you, but rather because your foolish brother has yet to prove himself."

Georgiana's mouth hung open for a moment, astonished that her brother had accepted such a responsibility so quickly. That was most unlike him—but, then again, he had changed significantly in almost every way since he had married Alice Jones.

"Therefore," her brother continued, his smile gentle, "therefore, you need not worry you will find no one to court you. *I* will do so on your behalf."

Something kicked hard at Georgiana's stomach. "What do you mean?" she asked quickly as her brother rose to his feet, smiling at her fondly. "What are your intentions, Allerton?"

He shrugged. "I will find you a suitable match, Georgiana, just as I arranged my match with Alice. That has turned out wonderfully well, you must admit, and I can only hope you will find a similar happiness with whomever it is that I choose for you."

Georgiana tried to say something in response, tried to open her mouth to protest that her brother did not need to go to such lengths, only to find that her lips were refusing to do as she intended. Allerton's smile remained on his face, his expression warm as he gave a contented sigh.

"I will ensure to consider at length the many gentlemen that might suit you," he said in a clear attempt to reassure her. "I will not be hasty nor will I simply make a match in order to suit myself. You need have no fear of that, my dear sister. I am not that sort of gentleman any longer, thanks to Alice."

"I know that to be true," Georgiana answered, surprised at just how thin her voice was, how tight her throat felt. "I will make sure to thank her also." She did not know what else to say, feeling as though she were being swept along in a fast-flowing river without any means of escape. Her brother was trying to do his best for her, she knew, but she had never wanted him to find her a match! She had enjoyed being able to meet and converse with the various gentlemen of the *ton,* although it had been a great disappointment when none of them had sought to take matters any further with her.

She smiled at her brother as he took his leave, giving her the day of their departure for London, but the smile did not speak of any true joy or happiness in her heart. Instead, she felt nothing more than fear and worry.

"I will let you return to your needlework," Lord Allerton said, reaching down to pat Georgiana's hand. "You need not look so fearful, my dear sister. It will all turn out very well indeed. I am sure of it."

"I thank you," Georgiana murmured as her brother walked from the room, feeling a sense of relief cloak her as the door closed. In the silence that followed, Georgiana was left with a myriad of thoughts and emotions, leaving her feeling quite overwhelmed.

"It may not be as bad as you fear," she told herself aloud, forcibly stemming the flood of tears that poured into her eyes. "You need not be afraid."

Georgiana swallowed hard, forcing her tears back and looking up the ceiling in an attempt to keep them at bay. Her brother *had* changed over this last year, and she was sure he would not make a match for her without asking for Alice's opinion—and Lady Allerton was both wise and considerate. And did she herself not want to marry? She had always longed for a husband and a home of her own, for that was every young lady's dream. That dream had felt very far away of late, but now, mayhap, it would be fulfilled, even if she herself had not made the choice of who to marry. She had seen plenty of marriages of convenience, plenty young ladies thrown into their future without any consideration for their feelings on the matter, and she ought to be grateful that her brother would not be that way inclined. He would be careful, considerate, and, hopefully, wise in his choice.

All she had to do was prepare herself to meet her future husband, no matter who he might be.

CHAPTER ONE

"And here we are."

Georgiana pressed her hands together as she held them in her lap, looking out of the window as though seeing the townhouse would help her calm her nerves. She threw a quick glance towards her sister-in-law, seeing how Lady Allerton smiled back at her without any worry in her eyes. That was how Georgiana wished to be: free of all anxiety and, therefore, happy, contented and settled.

It was not how she felt at present.

"Your brother will do all he can to help find you a suitable match, Georgiana." Alice's voice, lilting with the American accent that had taken Georgiana some time to become used to. "But I will be here too. You know that, I hope."

"I do, of course," Georgiana answered, seeing the kindness in Lady Allerton's smile and feeling it soothe her fractious thoughts. "I would be glad for your input when it comes to my brother's decisions, Alice. He may well choose someone he believes will be entirely suitable and, whilst they will appear to be so with their good title, excellent fortune, and perfect family line, they might fall short in their character."

"Which I quite understand," Lady Allerton said with a small sigh and a slight shake of her head that betrayed just how well she understood Georgiana's dilemma. "Your brother has a good heart, Georgiana. He means well, but his considerations do not always have much of an...emotive nature. As you have just said, he thinks mostly of family lines, of titles and wealth."

"Which mean very little," Georgiana muttered, sitting back in her carriage seat and sighing heavily. "Although I should not wish to marry a pauper."

"No, indeed not," Lady Allerton chuckled as the carriage came to a stop. "That would cause a good many difficulties indeed!"

Georgiana sighed again, shivering just a little as the carriage door was opened. The drive to London had taken some time, and even with the hot bricks, their multiple blankets, and their many stops, it was still cold in the carriage. She would be glad to get inside and to sit in front of a roaring fire for a time.

Once inside, Georgiana threw aside any suggestion of resting in her bedchamber and made her way directly to the drawing-room. Her brother had ridden to London a day earlier than they and had ensured the house was prepared for their arrival. There was a warm fire waiting for her in the drawing-room and Georgiana hurried towards it, her hands outstretched and desperate for the warmth.

"Ah, Georgiana, there you are!"

She let out a small shriek, spinning around to see her brother sitting in an armchair close to the fire. He chuckled good-naturedly, getting up out of his chair and making for the door, ready to greet his wife.

"I did not see you there," she stammered as he grinned. "You arrived safely, then?"

"I did," he said just as Lady Allerton came into the room. "And here is my dear wife." Embracing her warmly, Georgiana looked away, a little embarrassed to be watching such a display of affection, and yet, at the same time, there came a pang of longing. A longing she too might find such happiness and love for herself. Her brother and Alice's marriage had been one of arrangement, not one that had come from any sort of emotion yet, a love had been borne from it. A love that was evident every day. That was the sort of love Georgiana wanted for herself—and just because her marriage would be one of arrangement did not mean there was no chance for such a thing to occur.

"You will be glad to know, Georgiana, that I have already found two suitable gentlemen for you to meet," her brother said, drawing Lady Allerton along with him as he walked back towards the center of the room. "I am sure you will think very highly of them both."

Georgiana exchanged a quick glance with Lady Allerton before smiling at her brother. "I thank you," she told him with as much fervor as she could manage. "You have been working hard on my behalf, and I am truly grateful." Seeing how her brother smiled, she spread out her hands in a questioning gesture. "Might I inquire as to their names?"

"But of course!" Lord Allerton exclaimed as the door opened to allow in two maids who set down trays of refreshments and a slightly steaming pot of tea that caught both Georgiana and Lady Allerton's eye almost at once. "One is Lord Tolliver, who is a Viscount with excellent holdings, whilst the other is the Earl of Pembrokeshire."

Lady Allerton frowned. "The Earl of Pembrokeshire?" she repeated as her husband nodded fervently. "Is he not the very same gentleman who had to deal with the consequences of what was a terrible scandal in the summer?"

Georgiana's stomach dropped to the floor as she looked at her brother, seeing how he winced.

"He is the very same," he admitted to his wife. "I have to speak to him about that particular matter and, of course, if I find such a thing to be true, then there will be no—"

"Allerton!" Lady Allerton was staring at her husband, her eyes flashing and one hand curled into a fist. "You cannot push your poor sister towards a gentleman who has been accused of attempting to elope with the daughter of a Duke simply so he might find a little more financial stability in the long term."

Georgiana's eyes flared wide as she looked from her brother to Lady Allerton and back again. Had her brother honestly thought that such a gentleman would be suitable for her?

"There may be no truth to it," Lord Allerton said

hastily, holding up his hands defensively. "I will speak to Lord Pembrokeshire and discover whether or not it has even a small hint of truth about it."

"And if it does?" Lady Allerton demanded, sounding quite upset with her husband. "What then?"

Lord Allerton began to stammer, and Georgiana could not help but smile. It seemed her brother was not going to be able to make any foolish decisions given the strength of his wife, and for that, she was very glad indeed.

"Of course, I shall not make any agreement with Lord Pembrokeshire if I discover those rumors to have any basis in truth," he said firmly, which only took a little fire from Lady Allerton's eyes. "You need not worry, my dear. I shall be very careful indeed."

Lady Allerton sniffed, lifted her chin, and fixed her husband with an icy gaze. "Be sure you are," she told him, sternly, as Georgiana watched with a mixture of both amusement and relief. "For I shall not permit Georgiana to marry anyone with such a reputation."

Lord Allerton cleared his throat, gesturing for them all to sit down. Lady Allerton poured the tea, handing Georgiana a cup before sitting down herself and looking expectantly at her husband, clearly thinking he had more to say.

"You will need some new gowns, of course," Lord Allerton said as Georgiana nodded eagerly. "The winter is to be a very cold one indeed, or so I am told, although the frost has not been lingering for too much of the day as yet."

Georgiana nodded, sipping her tea and closing her

eyes at the wonderful warmth that began to spread through her. After the long and arduous journey in the cold carriage, she finally felt as though she were becoming warm again. "I thank you, Allerton," she told her brother. "I will need a new cloak also, I believe, not because there is any need for me to cling to the latest fashions, but merely because I—"

"You shall have whatever you please for whatever reason you may want it," her brother interrupted with a charming smile in her direction as if he were trying to make up for his foolishness only some moments before. "You know very well that things are much improved when it comes to financial matters, and thus, I am very happy indeed to pay for whatever you require."

A sudden urge to go out into London again hit Georgiana hard and, as she sipped her tea again, she glanced towards Lady Allerton. The lady herself might be too tired to join her, but surely there was a maid she could take as a chaperone?

"Might I go to a few shops this afternoon?" she asked, making her brother look up in surprise. "I know we have only just arrived, and there cannot be long until the dark evenings begin to creep in on us, but I should very much like to take a stroll through London."

Her brother made to shake his head, only to catch a sharp glance from his wife. "I—yes, of course," he stammered a little awkwardly. "I will attend with you, shall I? Not that I have any intention of looking at ribbons or the like, but rather that I would walk with you if you would wish it. Although I would prefer to take the carriage, of course."

"Then the carriage it shall be," Georgiana shrugged, thinking to herself she would not mind taking the carriage if it meant she could wander in and out of the shops that offered so many wonderful things. "Shall we say, within the hour?"

Her brother sighed heavily, although a teasing smile caught the corner of his mouth. "Within the hour," he agreed, finally managing to earn a warm look from his wife, which seemed to please him greatly. "And we will ensure to purchase you a new cloak at least, for you cannot go about London without such a thing."

"I will make sure to do so," Georgiana answered, setting her teacup down and rising to her feet. "If you will excuse me, I will go to prepare for our departure."

THE LONDON SHOPS were everything Georgiana remembered them to be, although the damp, cold weather did seem to lessen their appeal just a little. In the summertime, one could walk along the street and see windows covered in bright colors, with ribbons displayed in one window and a new bonnet in another. Now, however, in the gloom of the day, it felt as though there were a drabness to the ribbons and a dullness to the bonnets that had not been there before. But Georgiana felt quite contented in herself regardless, smiling warmly at every shopkeeper she saw.

A new cloak was purchased without too much difficulty, and Georgiana knew it would keep her very warm indeed. She purchased a new muffler in another shop and then some ribbons in the third. The gowns and the like would have to wait until another day, of course, but the joy of being back in London again filled Georgiana's soul, even when it began to rain.

"The carriage is a little away still, my dear," her brother said, looking glumly up at the sky. "We might go into this bookshop for a moment until the rain begins to lessen?"

A sudden thundering caught Georgiana unexpectedly, making her gasp in fright as the sound rolled across the sky, making everything else fall entirely silent. It faded away completely, only for the skies to open and the rain to pour with such intensity that Georgiana felt it soaking through her bonnet almost at once.

Her brother did not hesitate but practically pushed her in through the door of the bookshop, hurrying in himself after her. A flash of lightning lit up the sky, making her gasp with fright as she pressed both hands to her hammering heart, feeling both awestruck and afraid in equal measure.

"Good afternoon," she heard her brother say, turning her head to see him speak to the proprietor. "We will have to linger in your shop a while, I fear, but I will make sure to purchase a few books from you."

The proprietor did not look to be at all disturbed by this remark, inclining his head towards Lord Allerton. "But of course," came the reply. "You must wait for as long as is necessary. This thunder should pass soon, I'd expect, but the rain..." he trailed off, and Georgiana looked back out of the window, seeing how the rain practically bounced off the pavement and the cobbles of the street. It was quite a downpour!

"You must find at least one book to purchase, Georgiana," her brother said, his voice low as he came towards her. "It is only fair."

She laughed, the fear and unease of the thunderstorm finally fading away. "I can find more than one," she told him teasingly. "I will have at least five by the time our carriage arrives and the rain has died away."

Her brother arched one eyebrow, but Georgiana laughed and turned away, letting her eyes drift along the stacked shelves of books in the hope she might find a new novel of some kind with which she might occupy herself for a time. She was not a great reader by any means, which, most likely, her brother knew, but she would certainly be able to pull out a few books to purchase to take home. The winter meant there were undoubtedly fewer afternoon calls and the like that would entertain her, so she might perhaps finish even three novels by the time Christmas came.

Her heart lifted at the thought of Christmas. She had already enjoyed one Christmas with her brother and his new wife, and it had been such a wonderful occasion, she was looking forward to this year with an even greater sense of anticipation. There would be the singing of carols, the greenery brought into the house, the mistletoe and the holly berries that made her heart swell with the sheer joy of the Christmas season. There would be gifts to give and celebrations to enjoy. Georgiana was quite certain it would be just as lovely as the previous year... although whether or not she would be engaged by then, she had very little idea. There was only one month until Christmas Day, but that was long enough for her brother to make an agreement with whatever gentleman he settled on.

Just so long as it is not Lord Pembrokeshire, she thought to herself, grimly. *Even Alice knows he is not suitable!*

Another thunderclap caught her off guard, making her jump as a small exclamation left her mouth. A little embarrassed, she clamped one hand over her mouth, praying that no one had heard her.

"I was a little frightened too."

Her cheeks heated furiously as she turned her head to see a gentleman looking at her, a small smile lifting his mouth as his eyes fixed on her. He was standing a short distance away, at the end of a shelf of books, and as she watched him, he came around to her, drawing a little closer. Her heart squeezed tight for a moment, realizing she did not know this gentleman and, as such, she should not engage with him.

"Are you hiding from the rain?" the gentleman asked, his accent capturing her attention. "I confess I'm having to do the same."

"You...you are from America," Georgiana said before realizing what she was saying. Flushed, she dropped her head. "Forgive me," she stammered, daring a glance up at the gentleman. "I did not mean to—"

"Please, please." The gentleman was chuckling, his hands held up. "You needn't worry. But yes, you are correct. I am from Boston." He bowed deeply. "Mr. Oliver Lowell."

Georgiana dipped into a curtsy, aware her cheeks were still a little red. This was not at all the correct procedure, and certainly her brother would think her very improper to be continuing to converse with a gentleman who had not yet been properly introduced to her but, given the circumstances, and given he was from an entirely different country, Georgiana decided to continue as she was.

"I am glad to make your acquaintance," she said quietly, a little relieved the sound of the rain on the roof quietened her voice all the more. "I am Lady Georgiana, sister to the Earl of Allerton."

The gentleman blinked in surprise, perhaps unused to such high titles. "I see," he said after a moment. "Well, Lady Georgiana, I hope to see you again while I'm here in London. I came to visit a cousin and should be here for a few weeks still." A shoulder lifted in a half shrug. "I haven't decided if I'll stay here for Christmas or not. I guess I'll have to wait and see how things go."

Georgiana, unused to having a stranger speak so openly to her, smiled a little cautiously, taking the gentleman in. He was not overly tall, although half a head taller than herself, with a broad frame and a thick head of dark brown hair. His appearance was pleasing, with hazel eyes, ruddy cheeks, and a lopsided smile that seemed to add to his charm. His speech, however, was very dissimilar to that of the *ton,* and his manner, of course, was certainly very different to what she might expect. Not that she held it against him, of course, for she knew very well just how difficult it had been for her sister-in-law.

"I hail from Boston," he continued, making Georgiana realize there had been a silence for a moment or two that had added a slight sense of strain between them. "Although my cousin removed here a few years ago."

"I see," Georgiana answered, politely. "My brother recently married, and his wife comes from America also." She smiled as his expression became one of astonishment. "That is why I recognized your accent."

Mr. Lowell blinked rapidly, then shook his head in evident surprise. "Well, that's wonderful to hear, Lady Georgiana," he said. "It can be difficult to fit into London society, but if your sister-in-law has managed to do so, then I must hope that I will be welcomed also."

"I am sure you will be," she answered with a quick smile. "Might I inquire as to the name of your cousin?"

"Oh, yes, of course. She is Lady Rutledge, married to Viscount Rutledge. They have an estate but they do spend a considerable time here in London."

"Oh." Georgiana searched her memory to see if she had ever been introduced to Lord and Lady Rutledge but found she could not recall their names nor their faces. "I hope to meet them during the little Season, then," she said, covering her lack of knowledge of them. "And I am sure you will find yourself warmly welcomed into society also." Knowing it was time for her to remove herself from the conversation for propriety's sake, she inclined her head and took a step away from him, seeing out of the corner of her eye how he bowed and then turned away. At least he understood certain manners expected within society, she thought to herself, seeing how her brother emerged from another part of the bookshop, one book in his hand.

"You have nothing to read!" he exclaimed, mockingly exasperated. "I thought you were to take five!"

She rolled her eyes at him. "I thought to ask the proprietor to find me a new novel or two," she answered by way of excuse. "I shall do precisely that, should you be willing to wait for a few minutes?"

Lord Allerton sighed heavily, although his eyes twinkled. "Do be quick, Georgiana. The rain is beginning to lessen, and I would like to make for the carriage before it begins to pour again."

"Of course." She smiled and hurried towards the counter, seeing the proprietor looking up at her expectantly. She would have to tell Lady Allerton of her new acquaintance once she returned home. No doubt there would be a good many questions about him, and mayhap Lady Allerton herself would be glad to be introduced to Mr. Lowell. It might bring her some happiness to speak to a fellow countryman.

Thus contented, Georgiana allowed the proprietor to find her not one, but two new novels, her thoughts entirely on the task at hand and no longer settled on her new acquaintance, Mr. Lowell. Although she did not know the same could not be said for him.

CHAPTER TWO

Oliver could not help but watch the lovely young lady hurry from the bookshop, seeing what he presumed was a footman hurrying from the carriage with an umbrella held out for her. The rain had become a drizzle in the last few minutes, and both she and the gentleman she had been with had taken the chance to hurry to the carriage. He chuckled to himself, turning around as the carriage rolled away. She had been very lovely indeed, but he certainly had surprised her in some way or another.

Quite what he had done, he did not know, but there were certainly a good many aspects of London society he had not yet quite grasped. The news that there was another American here in London brought a fresh sense of happiness to his heart, for whilst he had been enjoying his time here, it did bring with it a small loneliness that often pervaded his otherwise contented life. His cousin and her husband had been more than welcoming and, whilst he had not yet attended any large social gatherings, there had been a small dinner and another soiree he had enjoyed, and he had been to the theatre twice so far. Margaret, his cousin, had been very glad to see him and had gently guided him forward when he had mis-stepped, whilst her husband had merely waved a hand and told Oliver not to worry.

Oliver could not help but look forward to his first London ball, given he had never attended such a thing before. It was to be tomorrow evening, if he recalled correctly, and he could not help but feel a small twinge of excitement as he considered it. Would Lady Georgiana be there? Would he have the opportunity to dance with her? Oliver was not quite sure what to do when it came to dancing, or even how to ask a lady to dance with him, but one thing was for certain—he intended to speak to Lady Georgiana again.

"Are you purchasing these, sir?"

Oliver set down the first three books on the counter and smiled at the proprietor, who looked at him quizzically.

"I would like to," he said with a grin, "but I wonder if you can tell me what sort of book that young lady might like."

The older man blinked slowly, tilting his head just a little to one side. "Young lady, sir?"

"The one who just left," Oliver said gesturing towards the door as though that would remind the fellow. "Lady Georgiana, I think. She was with a gentle-man." He looked back at the proprietor, aware of the slightly wary look in his eyes. Was he doing something wrong?

"You are speaking of Lady Georgiana," the proprietor said slowly. "She was with Lord Allerton, her brother."

Oliver nodded, a little cheered by the proprietor's seeming willingness to continue the conversation. "I should like to know what sort of book she would like," he said, wondering if he was making himself unclear in any way. "She was very kind to me and has informed me that her sister-in-law is also from America, as I am." He shrugged as the proprietor nodded slowly. "I'd like to send her a book that I hope she will enjoy, just as a gesture of thanks."

A look of understanding flooded the proprietor's face, and his smile spread, making Oliver sigh with relief.

"Ah, I quite understand, sir," the man answered, now looking quite happy to help Oliver with his intentions. "It is a very kind gesture, I am sure, and I know she will appreciate it. I helped her to find one or two new books just before she left, so if you wish, I could find another book of the same kind?"

Oliver nodded, leaning one elbow on the counter. "Please," he said gesturing to the bookshelves with his other hand. "That would be very helpful indeed." He smiled to himself as the proprietor hurried off, murmuring under his breath as he went.

At least that is one thing I have managed to do correctly, he thought to himself as the proprietor continued to scurry here and there between the shelves of books. *Sending a book to a lady as a gesture of thanks is obviously quite well thought of!* His broad smile remained as the proprietor came back to the counter with three books in his hands. He laid them out for Oliver to peruse, telling him these were some of the newer novels, and he was sure the lady would be glad to have any of them.

"Send all of them!" Oliver exclaimed on a whim, thinking he would make himself very proper indeed if he were to send three instead of one. "That way she will know just how thankful I am to have met her."

The proprietor goggled at him for a moment, looking at him in evident confusion before shaking his head and muttering to himself under his breath. Oliver frowned, wondering if he had been overeager, only to shrug inwardly and turn his head away. He was merely expressing his thankfulness through a kind gesture, and surely there was nothing that could be said about that!

"I shall have them sent directly," the proprietor said, glancing outside at the rain. "Just as soon as the rain has stopped, so the books do not get damaged."

Oliver nodded in understanding. "Thank you," he said. "I shall pay you and then be on my way."

WHEN OLIVER GOT BACK to the house, the rain had finally stopped, and the sun was attempting to shine through the clouds, although Oliver was not sure it would last.

"Good gracious!" his cousin cried as he stepped into the house. "Whatever happened to you?"

Oliver looked down at himself, seeing the glistening beads of rain running down his coat. "I am a little damp," he said with a shrug. "The hackneys were hard to find."

Lady Rutledge rolled her eyes. "They are not at all

hard to find," she said with a shake of her head. "You need only wave a hand, and one will come to you."

"They were entirely absent from the street!" he protested, handing his hat and gloves to the waiting butler whilst his cousin wrinkled her nose at the water that sprinkled from him as he took off his coat. "I tried my best, of course. I just hope the books I have sent to a lady will have been delivered to her without any difficulty."

His cousin, who had been about to walk away, stopped and turned to face him again. Her dark hair was pulled neatly back from her face, a few ringlet curls around her ears, but her brown eyes were wide with surprise, her mouth a perfect circle.

"What's wrong?" he asked, coming towards her and letting a grin settle on his face. "Is there something the matter?"

Lady Rutledge blinked rapidly, her lips pressing together tightly for a moment. "You sent a book to a lady?" she asked quietly, sounding a little surprised. "To whom?"

He shrugged, not wanting to make much of it. "I met a lady in the bookshop and she spoke very kindly to me. I have even discovered she has a sister-in-law from America!" This exclamation was met with a swift intake of breath, although Oliver did not know why such a thing should distress his cousin so. "Lady Georgiana, if I remember correctly. As a gesture of my thanks for her kindness today, I sent her three books."

A squeak came from his cousin's mouth. "Three?" she whispered, one hand pressed to her mouth, the word muffled behind her fingers. "You sent Lady Georgiana *three* books?"

"Yes," he said a little confused. "Whatever is wrong with that?"

Lady Rutledge closed her eyes tightly, her breathing still obviously a little quick. "Pray tell me how you came to be acquainted with her."

"I—I introduced myself to her," Oliver said as Lady Rutledge let out another exclamation of evident horror. "Why? Whatever is the matter?"

Lady Rutledge let out a long, slow breath and opened her eyes. "My dear cousin, how many times must I tell you that things are very different here in London?"

"You have told me many times," he admitted with a shrug. "But I cannot see what I have done now that is so intolerable."

"You do not introduce yourself to a complete stranger, especially if she is a young lady!" Lady Rutledge cried, throwing her hands up in evident exasperation. "I am sure I have told you such a thing before!"

Oliver shook his head slowly. "No, you haven't," he said firmly. "You or your husband have always been the ones to make the introductions, but I have never known that I should not introduce myself otherwise."

Her face began to turn a dusky shade of pink as Lady Rutledge groaned loudly. "I am sure I have done so," she said firmly. "But not only that, one does not send *three* books to a young lady so soon after their first meeting!"

Growing all the more frustrated, Oliver shook his head in exasperation. "Why does the number of books make any difference?" he asked, wishing he could throw up his hands as she had done. "I wanted to express my thanks at her kindness and for the happiness that was brought by her telling me of her sister-in-law. I cannot see what the problem was with me doing that!"

"Because *one* would have been appropriate!" Lady Rutledge cried, clearly very upset. "One book, one gift, one expression of thanks. Three books is much too overt, Lowell! It will suggest to her much more than a simple thanks."

Oliver swallowed hard, a cold hand grasping his heart. "What do you mean?"

"She will think you are interested in furthering your acquaintance with her!"

"But I am," he said a little confused. "I would very much like to speak to her again. I was hoping she would be willing to dance with me at the ball tomorrow evening."

Lady Rutledge groaned again and put her head in her hands. "You do not understand," she said as though Oliver did not know that already. "To send three books suggests a fondness, Lowell. A regard for her—and not only is such a thing inappropriate for someone you have only just met, but it is highly unorthodox."

Pressing his lips together hard, Oliver let out a long, heavy sigh and tried not to let this sudden uncomfortable sensation overwhelm him. He had never once thought that a gift of three books would suggest anything other than thanks, but now, it seemed, it would say far too much to Lady Georgiana.

"And you cannot simply go up to her and ask her to dance with you at the ball," Lady Rutledge continued in a warning voice. "You must be properly introduced, both to Lady Georgiana and then to Lord and Lady Allerton before you can even *think* of asking to sign her dance card, Lowell."

Sighing heavily, Oliver admitted defeat. "Very well," he said heavily, aware of the large space in between his standing in society and that of Lady Georgiana. "So you are suggesting that I might not be able to dance with her, then."

"I cannot say," Lady Rutledge muttered with a shake of her head. "After what you have done thus far, I cannot pretend the lady herself, as well as Lord Allerton, will not be affected by it. They might consider you to be a little too improper for their acquaintance."

Closing his eyes, Oliver felt a rush of homesickness overtake him. He wanted to return to the life he understood and to the customs that were entirely familiar to him. He had been in London for a few weeks now, and whilst he enjoyed many things there, the expectations and the demands of society were something he could not quite grasp.

"Do not think too much on it," Lady Rutledge said, stepping forward to put one hand on his arm as her eyes shone with a sudden sympathy, perhaps realizing she had been a little too harsh. "I should not have railed at you so. I know you were only trying to express thankfulness to Lady Georgiana, and I am glad she has spoken to you of her sister-in-law."

Oliver swallowed hard, feeling more foolish than ever before. "I would like to be introduced to Lady Allerton still," he told his cousin, seeing how she nodded. "If she refuses my acquaintance, then so be it, but given she is from the same country as I, then I can only hope she will forgive me."

Lady Rutledge smiled tightly but nodded. "I am sure she will understand," she said with more warmth in her voice. "Lady Allerton made quite a stir when she first appeared in London. She knows how difficult it can be. I think, despite what I have said at first, you will have nothing to fear."

A little relieved, Oliver nodded, patted his cousin's hand, and let out a long, heavy breath. "I thank you," he said, using the words that his cousin had taught him to say instead of a simple 'thanks.' "I don't mean to embarrass you in any way. I am sorry if I've managed to do that inadvertently."

Lady Rutledge sighed, but her smile remained intact. "We will manage, I am quite sure," she said with a wry look in her eyes. "Just ensure you stay close to myself or Lord Rutledge tomorrow evening. That way, we should be able to make quite certain you do nothing to shock the *beau monde*." A quiet laugh escaped her as she pressed his arm for a moment and then turned away. "Come, let us take some refreshment in the drawing-room. You will need something warm to drink after being in that downpour, and I certainly could do with a refreshing cup of tea."

Grateful to her for her kindness, Oliver followed without question, praying silently that Lady Georgiana would think just as well of him despite his mistake. The ball no longer held the same sense of appeal; the thought of being in her company again no longer as delightful. He swallowed hard as he walked into the drawing-room, feeling a sense of embarrassment capture him all over again. Hopefully, it would have faded by tomorrow evening, else Oliver was not at all sure how he would manage to make it through the evening! The last thing he wanted was to rush away in a flurry of shame and ruin his standing—as little as it was—within London society.

I will make sure to stick by Lady Rutledge, he told himself as she asked him to ring the bell for tea. *And then surely, nothing else will go wrong!*

WHAT WILL HAPPEN with Oliver and Georgiana? Will Oliver's mistakes create a scandal? Check out Mistletoe Magic on the Kindle store! Mistletoe Magic: A Regency Romance

Don't forget that it is a part of a multi author series, called Home for Christmas. Here is the link to the series page!

Home for Christmas Series Page

MY DEAR READER

Thank you for reading and supporting my books! I hope this story brought you some escape from the real world into the always captivating Regency world. A good story, especially one with a happy ending, just brightens your day and makes you feel good! If you enjoyed the book, would you leave a review on Amazon? Reviews are always appreciated.

Below is a complete list of all my books! Why not click and see if one of them can keep you entertained for a few hours?

The Duke's Daughters Series
The Duke's Daughters: A Sweet Regency Romance
Boxset
A Rogue for a Lady
My Restless Earl
Rescued by an Earl
In the Arms of an Earl
The Reluctant Marquess (Prequel)

A Smithfield Market Regency Romance
The Smithfield Market Romances: A Sweet Regency
Romance Boxset
The Rogue's Flower

Saved by the Scoundrel
Mending the Duke
The Baron's Malady

The Returned Lords of Grosvenor Square
The Returned Lords of Grosvenor Square: A Regency
Romance Boxset
The Waiting Bride
The Long Return
The Duke's Saving Grace
A New Home for the Duke

The Spinsters Guild
A New Beginning
The Disgraced Bride
A Gentleman's Revenge
A Foolish Wager
A Lord Undone

Convenient Arrangements
A Broken Betrothal
In Search of Love
Wed in Disgrace
Betrayal and Lies
A Past to Forget
Engaged to a Friend

Landon House
Mistaken for a Rake
A Selfish Heart
A Love Unbroken

A Christmas Match
A Most Suitable Bride
An Expectation of Love

Second Chance Regency Romance
Loving the Scarred Soldier
Second Chance for Love
A Family of her Own
A Spinster No More

Soldiers and Sweethearts
To Trust a Viscount
Whispers of the Heart
Dare to Love a Marquess
Healing the Earl
The Lady's Brave Heart

Christmas Stories
Love and Christmas Wishes: Three Regency Romance
Novellas
A Family for Christmas
Mistletoe Magic: A Regency Romance
Home for Christmas Series Page

Happy Reading!
All my love,
Rose

Printed in Great Britain
by Amazon

57858151R00121